SAUCE

02:29

International Bestselling Author
John A. Andrews

SAUCE

Copyright © 2022 by John A. Andrews.
All rights reserved. Written permission must be secured from the publisher to use or reproduce any part of this book, except for brief quotations in critical reviews or articles.
Published in the U.S.A. by
Books That Will Enhance Your Life™
A L I - Andrews Leadership International
www.JohnAAndrews.com
Cover Design: John A. Andrews
Cover Graphic Designer: A L I
Cover Photo: A L I
Edited by: A L I
ISBN: 9798835817047

SAUCE

TABLE OF CONTENTS

CHAPTER ONE..6
CHAPTER TWO..9
CHAPTER THREE...12
CHAPTER FOUR..15
CHAPTER FIVE..18
CHAPTER SIX...22
CHAPTER SEVEN...25
CHAPTER EIGHT...29
CHAPTER NINE..32
CHAPTER TEN...38
CHAPTER ELEVEN..43
CHAPTER TWELVE..48
CHAPTER THIRTEEN..51
CHAPTER FOURTEEN..54
CHAPTER FIFTEEN...58
CHAPTER SIXTEEN...62
CHAPTER SEVENTEEN...67
CHAPTER EIGHTEEN..70
CHAPTER NINETEEN..73
CHAPTER TWENTY..75
CHAPTER TWENTY-ONE..78
CHAPTER TWENTY-TWO..82
CHAPTER TWENTY-THREE..87
CHAPTER TWENTY-FOUR...92
CHAPTER TWENTY-FIVE...97
CHAPTER TWENTY-SIX...100
CHAPTER TWENTY-SEVEN.......................................105
CHAPTER TWENTY-EIGHT.......................................108
CHAPTER TWENTY-NINE..112
CHAPTER THIRTY...115
CHAPTER THIRTY-ONE...119
CHAPTER THIRTY-TWO...125
CHAPTER THIRTY-THREE.......................................129
CHAPTER THIRTY-FOUR..133
CHAPTER THIRTY-FIVE..137
CHAPTER THIRTY-SIX...141
CHAPTER THIRTY-SEVEN.......................................144
CHAPTER THIRTY-EIGHT.......................................149
CHAPTER THIRTY-NINE..153

SAUCE

"David touches the box.
Lifts it.
Oblivious to him, the freezer shook."

SAUCE

SAUCE

02:29

SAUCE

1

Halloween 2015 had come and gone. Kids have long forgotten about the tricks and treats and even the costumes they wore. Grownups, no doubt had taken their costumes to the dry cleaners, picked them up, stored them in the clothes closet, or even inside boxes way up in the attic. Christmas elapsed after Santa Claus came down the grimy cobwebbed chimney and filled stockings of all sizes and textures.

SAUCE

The new year stepped up to the plate with a bang and batted. Another leap year? Yes! They drop every four years. It's a year, having 366 days including February 29 as an intercalary day. On that day we find ourselves in Morristown.

Morristown is a historic city seated in Morris County, New Jersey, United States. Known for its strategic role in the war for American independence from Great Britain it has been dubbed "the military capital of the American Revolution." Its wartime makeup is reflected in eclectic attractions including the Morristown National Historical Park and the picturesque Vail Mansion.

It is said: *If it's the end of October in Morristown, you can guarantee (hurricanes and unseasonable snowstorms notwithstanding) there will be Halloween festivities for the entire community.*

At this once-a-year event in late October, Judges customarily look for the most original, scariest, and best-looking costumes with prizes going to winners in four age categories including Millennials and the famed Gen Z, a huge draw to the scariness of Halloween.

Nestled and semi-isolated in its Suburban community is a huge multi-level brown and tan building with Futura Bold fonts in block letters **Morristown College** etched close to its summit. An institution credited for attracting students for athletics, medicine, industry, and the arts. Subsequently, boasting state-of-the-art

SAUCE

lawn tennis, basketball, as well as track and field courts.

Its landscaping is not only amazing but immaculate with well-manicured green grass on top of petite hills and valleys, analogous to roller coasters and the city's wartime culture.

SAUCE

2

It is mid-afternoon on February 29th, 2016, just over one month after Donald John Trump was inaugurated as POTUS 45, and a few days after a roadside bomb hits a military convoy, killing six Turkish Army soldiers in the southeast Diyarbakır Province.

On that day as on most, a multi-demographic tranche of at least 60 Students mingled in its courtyard. Some touting textbooks. Some discuss athletic gear as well as

SAUCE

the latest sports news. While others pow-wow as if prepping for a Monologue Fest.

The school bell rings. Students saunter inside. Two lone security guards conduct their regular "after the bell" sweep, ensuring no slackers were lingering on the college grounds and/or around its perimeter.

One of its track and field elites is Megan Cantine, pronounced *Canteen* (meaning small cafeteria or snack bar) word descendants of the German *Kantine* and Turkish *Kantin*.

Megan, in a Bob-Cut hairstyle responding to the bell, not only comes beautifully groomed at age 21 but is a very talented sprinter with a record of **100 yards in 9.1 seconds** (close to the World Record of Jesse Owens in 9.4).

Megan, tailgating that hurried batch of students makes a pit-stop next to that large oak-wood-top administrative desk located at the beginning of that expansive hallway. There is a busy Administrative Attendant at this huge counter, shuffling papers, aided by two other individuals facilitating as peons. Restrooms for men and women opposed, prequels the huge desk.

Megan opens a Gucci purse, grabs her iPhone and after a few scrolls, she peers into the mirror. Not liking what she sees, Megan strides to the Women's restroom for the essential touch-up.

Moments later, after a toilet flush, she exits the stall. A sanitizing canister fixture near the sink highlights. She

SAUCE

accesses it for a cleanse. After disinfecting of hands, Megan faces her reflection in the square restroom mirror perched inches above the sink. Retrieving a stick of lip gloss from her purse she refreshes her lips and puckers them to ensure evenness of texture. Her phone rings. She trades the tube of lipgloss for the iPhone and answers.

SAUCE

3

After saying Hello, Megan questions herself as to the mysteriousness of the caller. Anyway, she continues the conversation, in a mindset of accommodating.
"Megan, is this you?"
The Male Voice asks cordially.
"Who is this?"
Asks Megan in response.
The Male Voice asks, not only in a commanding but a raspier tone.

SAUCE

"Who do you think it is?"
In Megan's psyche, curiosity peaks. She ponders. She looks on her cellphone screen and sees these two words displayed: Private Caller.
"I'm so tired of dealing with all of these prank calls. Hi Siri, who the hell is this?"
SIRI pronounced (SIRR-ee) the voice assistant for the Apple iPhone answers back:
"I am sorry. I am not sure I understand what you are trying to do."
Megan responds:
"Kill this SOB who is stalking me."
The Man's Voice, now in a commandingly over-the-top tone,
"How about the Son of a Bitch who is about to drink your blood and hang you out to dry?"
Instantaneously, Megan hears CLICK! The caller hangs up the phone.
Alarmed. Megan nervously returns the phone to her purse. Accidentally, the Phone falls to the ground. Panicking. She picks up the iPhone and secures it in her purse. Noticing her soiled hands, she turns on the faucet to wash them. The spigot sputters out a small supply of water, followed in tow by huge gusts of blood. Not only does the top of the sink get plastered with the blood but Megan gets doused in the process. She is terrified. She screams.
The Faucet's still running. Before Megan could attempt to turn off the flow of blood, she notices underneath

SAUCE

the door in the adjacent stall the image of two male feet wearing black sweat pants and red and black sneakers a size 12 plus.

Megan quivers. Blood from the spigot still sputtering on her, in haste her hand grabs the tap and she shuts off the faucet. Suddenly...she hears loud footsteps followed by the squeaking of door hinges and continued loud footsteps.

Megan bolts for the door. On her way, a Masked Form exits the stall. Peripherally, Megan sees a glittering dagger hoisted in Its hand and coming toward her.

She hustles.

It traps her.

It slices her on the left arm.

She bleeds.

It craves more stabbings.

Megan fights It off.

The door slams behind Megan.

It grabs the door, reopens it, and at top speed It jets out in pursuit of Megan.

SAUCE

Entering that spacious hallway, students and faculty seek refuge. While the administrative attendants hide underneath the huge oak desk, students clear out. They scurry to their classes and lock themselves behind those doors.
With the availability of space and clarity, It suddenly gains inches on Megan. She looks back in Its direction, momentarily. In Its eyes, she sees not only a monstrosity but a freak of nature, with a dark, lonely, deep, cluttered, and sinister soul.

SAUCE

The chase escalates onto the college grounds. The scream of the torpedoing Megan rose to a crescendo. Students clear out. The Masked Form closing in on Megan sees two intercepting Security Guards. It stabs them in their stomachs in succession and continues in the pursuit of Megan Cantine.

On sunny days like this at the college, many students after reporting to class tend to frequent the college grounds to catch up on schoolwork or chit-chat with other classmates in a semi-private setting. Others involved in athletics, occupy the varied available courts as part of their curriculum.

Suddenly, students begin to scatter. Those caught up in Its track are either stampeded or slashed with Its sharp dagger.

Mercedes Black, African American a knockout, with a shaved hairstyle in her early twenties, and carrying a large stack of books comes out from the side doors. She witnessed both slayings of the guards and is appalled as to what's unfolding right in front of her naked eyes. Meanwhile, many unleased students toss their textbooks and other articles at the Masked Form. Not Mercedes.

Precipitously Mercedes is startled by a shape wearing a mask. She screams out. Weak-handed Mercedes loses her grip on her books.

They spread the pavement, broadly.

She's pissed. Her reaction says she's not a happy camper on campus.

SAUCE

"What the F...Who the heck started this? Do you all know how much my textbooks cost? Take your scary ass tactics to another joint."
Instantly, Mercedes' classmate Ray in an upscale sweat-suit and designer sneakers removes the mask and bounces.
Mercedes goes ballistic.
"Ray! Don't play me. Are you trying to be a copycat or a fricking maniac? You need to get a life."
Ray bounces as he chuckles.
Even so, Mercedes refused to be separated from her books. She braces the wall with her rear end; to not only oversee possible looters but keep an eye on the Masked Form, Megan Cantine episode.
Students clear out from the path of the chase. Some pupils with their hands over their mouths in wonderment. Others are still laughing over the stunt Ray pulled on Mercedes.
The dust settles. Mercedes shakes her head in disgust, picks up her books, and returns through those doors that she had entered earlier.

SAUCE

5

Megan has been doused in her own blood, unknowingly. The students who know her well would say that in Megan's mind she would be thinking:
"No problem, I have bigger fish to fry - getting this monster off my back."
Salt-and-pepper hair like President Obama's, African American MR. SPIKES, aka Dean Spikes, in his mid-50s, emerges onto the scene from the same door

SAUCE

through which Mercedes exited and returned. He's a sporty dresser and the President of Morristown College for over twelve years. Sweating bricks of perspiration, he hustles to investigate the brewing melee, marinating on his turf and now looping the building. In a head-on collision, he bumps into the bloodied, terrified Megan.

They SCREAM out together.

In go mode, Megan accidentally wipes her bloodied hands on Spikes' face and his designer blazer. He masks his concern for his soiled gear as he avoids being run over by the Masked Form.

Several students standing on the side-line and noticing that almost close encounter between their Dean and The Masked Form, screams. Spikes makes an about-turn. Coincidentally, serving as a decoy, he winds up trailing The Masked Form and Megan.

The college grounds are blood-labeled and inundated with screams, tears, and indistinctive noises as the faculty spearheaded by Dean Spikes seek aid from this mayhem.

Spikes, yells,

"We need help! Somebody, please!"

Unfortunately, no one heeds the call.

In the distance sirens wail. Up close, multiple students, boys & girls, mingle and shielded by faculty, navigate to their classrooms. Their faces display a climate of fear reacting to the scary aftereffects. Their chatter is not only loud but reverberating and vindictive as well.

SAUCE

Meanwhile, The Masked Form PROWLS.

Megan sprinting, penetrates the crowd of stalled, and alarmed students, screaming bloody murder as The Masked Form inches on her. Students entering the conversation get SLASHED with Its weapon.

They BLEED.

One Student sticks a foot out attempting to trip the Masked Form. That student gets stabbed so deeply in the chest, that she croaks in a flash. Other students react by screaming their lungs out. That murderous pit-stop slows The Masked Form somewhat. However, It remains in pursuit.

Megan leaves some daylight between them but her feet accidentally SLIP on the grassy surface. Her Gucci purse sails then it falls to the ground. She recovers the accessory and rebounds quickly before she falls prey to The Masked Form. Even so, looking through the corner of her eyes, she sees The Masked Form gaining inches on her. Suddenly…

Swish!

It viscously stabs Megan in the chest with the dagger.

She FALLS. Her eyes roll displaying mostly white. It brutally pulls the knife out of her wound and tries another stab. Megan wards off his hand. His stabbing hand hits Megan hard in her wound. Feeling he still got a blow-in. He chuckles.

Megan bleeds.

She groans.

She trips.

SAUCE

She topples.
She collapses.
A loud blow.
Megan falls to the concrete, hard.
She hurts, badly.
She's down for the count.

SAUCE

Unpeeling onlookers flood the streets of halted vehicular traffic. With most of the abandoned college grounds in the backdrop, sirens wail in the distance. Vehicle horns blast continuously. Gridlock traffic turns the street into a parking lot. Up ahead an accident blocking both lanes contributes to the traffic mayhem. Emergency vehicles including Sheriff cars are stuck. While their flashing lights illume, the emission of greenhouse gases evaporates.

SAUCE

In the meantime, motorists vent, contributing to the escalating road rage. On the other hand, the frequent braking and accelerating of vehicles add to this traffic buildup. Motorists are discombobulated, distraught, and more seriously delayed.

Tangentially, The Masked Form sees Spikes trailing. It switches Its focus onto Spikes. The Dean takes off hastily, outwitting and eludes It, and hides behind a huge pillar.

The Masked form is in disarray. No Spikes? The Masked Form cools Its heels. With beaming eyes, It searches for Its next target.

Suddenly, the wind whistles.

Trees sway.

Debris soars.

Dogs howl

Students continually run for cover.

The Masked Form ambulates and stands alone momentarily. Suddenly Its head turns in the direction of those scattering students. It sees Megan in that crowd. It immediately returns in relentless pursuit of Its victim, Megan Cantine, with eyeballs protruding ominously underneath Its facial covering. Demolition emanates from inside those aqueous humors. Its body language spells: I've got to have her. Instantly It catches up with the gasping Megan.

They wrestle.

Megan punches It HARD in the face and abs. It shakes off the blows and attempts another stab but fails to

SAUCE

land.

Megan goes for Its jugular. It slips out of the punch.

Megan, not trusting Its fortitude, HUSTLES and almost collides with a brave, agile, muscular, Student. He shields her and takes It on like a brave soldier.

Swish! Swish! Swish!

The Shape's dagger indentations draw gushing blood from the three wounds in the Student's furbished chest. The student topples to the concrete and dies.

SAUCE

7

The environment is eerie, to say the least.
Whistling wind crescendo. Screams, as well as venting, fill the air, while the distant wailing of sirens contributes. Megan, after eluding The Masked Form during that last slaying of the student - senses her getaway.
In the backdrop, the digital calendar on the wall rattles. It reads 02: 29: 2016, tantamount to another leap year on the calendar.

SAUCE

Suddenly, the device ejects from the wall and sails through the college grounds like a torpedo, crashing into the head of the Masked Form.
It shakes off the blow. In Its path, the Masked Form eliminates two other students by stabbing them to death. After those two slayings, it eventually disappears.
Sirens wail as Emergency vehicles speedily cascade onto the college grounds. Thus creating a spectacle of confusion and fortissimo as the college goes into crisis mode. Students left for dead are wallowing in their pain, distress, and calamitous encounters. In the meantime, Spikes, still shaken up, oversees and consoles many ill-fated students as well as their venting parents.
Emerging from that crushed batch, and debunking the avenger with his hand fisted held and high is Afro hair styled DAVE SIMMONS, African American, scholarly with a British brogue and early 20s.
"We did nothing to deserve this. This evil Form must die! Evil shall never reign over good. Darkness over light. Never!"
Dave says.
News Reporters, press, and they salivate observing a plethora of dead bodies as well as onlookers. Sticking the microphone in Dave's face is Reporter, Michelle Myers in her 30s, with a Shag hairstyle, mixed ethnicity, and sophisticated demeanor.

SAUCE

"Sir, you too are feeling the effects of this onslaught. How...?"
Dave eluding the Reporter responds,
"Nothing to say now. This blood-sucker must die!"
"If there's a killer. He's got to have a motive for all of this. Or do we have a Serial Killer on our hands?
Six people are dead. Yet, no one has claimed responsibility. Is it the Masked Form, now at large who's directly responsible? Or could there be accomplices involved?
This is Michelle Myers from NEWS 8. More to come on this developing story."
Observing the bloodbath, Dean Spikes looks traumatized.
"Let's get some help for these ailing kids. In my 12 years as the provost, I have never witnessed such occurrences. Never! Morristown College has experienced such a major blow today."
Says Spikes.
In the meantime, Medics exit their vehicles. They aid with gurney support and trauma. The grounds are now filled with students desiring early dismissal. They VENT.
Even so, the college remains on lockdown.
Law enforcement finally arriving on the scene keeps them at bay. On the faces of parents and most onlookers, one could see only grief and heartbreak.
Environmentally. Human screams compete with sounds of sirens, vehicular horns, and multi-dialect

verbiage. A patchwork of hysteria and blood decorates the College compound.

News Reporter Caroline Beckles, a Caucasian in her 30s is tasked. She presses as her cameraman greenlights.

Caroline, somewhat frenzied reports,

"Call it what it is. This is a darn bloodbath.

Oh, there's a cop when you need one, with his body cam to boot."

The Sheriff's cruiser bears down.

BRAKES SCREECH

The Driver's door swings open.

Out steps the bald surveying African American Sheriff Chief Thomas Chase in his 50s. He's a by-the-book cop. His radio chatters loudly.

Chase responds,

"Lock it down. Close off all entrances and exits! Nobody leaves. Anyone entering this crime scene must be thoroughly vetted."

A voice on the radio transmits:

"Copy that. Over!"

SAUCE

Sheriff Chase dives deep into the investigating process with a sense of urgency.

Instantly, he blends in with the crowded blood-covered milieu of locals. They evaluate the disaster as well as pester Chase for arriving late onto the scene. He eyeballs them as he listens to their accounts. He buoys. Additional Sheriffs as backup units bear down on the scene. The squealing brakes, slamming car doors and loud dispatch radio chatter validate the strong

SAUCE

presence of law enforcement.

With his chest stuck out. Sheriff Chase has cleverly eluded the News Reporters and become duty-bound. Gray-haired Claude Jackson, an Onlooker in his 60s presses. He eyes the time on his Apple wristwatch. Claude wants more.

"What kind of Sheriff's Department is this?"

Claude, eyeing the Sheriff's badge exclaims:

"Late is a darn ugly four-letter word! Trying to close the gate when the wolf has already devoured the sheep and exited? Sheriff Chase, you better find that monster swiftly and bring him to justice. You, hear me? Blue lives matter. Black lives matter. All lives matter…We want Justice for these kids and their families!"

Suddenly, brakes squeal followed by a slammed car door. Black hair with tan highlights and darting out of her black pickup truck, Sissey Cantine mid- 50s, mixed ethnicity, a boss-woman, sandbags onto the scene. Sissey inadvertently points fingers.

"Where is my Megan?"

Thomas Chase is all ears. He ambulates and lands inside Sissey Cantine's thickening huddle of supporters. Loud chatter emanates from that crowd. Thomas Chase, with one eye on the crowd and the other on surveillance, asks:

"Could there be others like him in the student body? Or what about even outside copycats?"

The Sheriff continues in demand:

SAUCE

"We need to seal this place down immediately."
Multiple Sheriff Officers dart to a parked cruiser. The trunk pops open. They access yellow tape and begin to seal off the crime scene.
Sheriff Chase focusing on Sissey Cantine asks:
"Parent...?"
Sissey turns away while she refrains from answering.

SAUCE

9

Through the multi-ethnic suburbs of Morristown, Sheriff cruisers continually PATROL streets. The on-roof cruiser lights illume as they rotate. Parents are drawn into the surveillance debacle. Most are in disarray while they circulate flyers depicting The Masked Form's monstrosity.

A venting black woman wearing a white head-tie and in her 60s, Virginia Michaels is handed a flyer. After

SAUCE

absorbing its contents, she comes to grips with herself and becomes an advocate for the cause.
"This is for real!"
She pleads.
Multiple parents are still in doubt.
"Doubting Thomas(s)"
She exclaims.
Virginia takes the flyer to her house on the hill. Upon entering, the door opens from the inside. Exiting the house in dreadlocks is her daughter Grace Michaels. She has a Rastafarian swagger and is in her late 30s. Grace had watched the distribution process of flyers from the living room window.
"Mom, don't believe everything you hear. Believe what you see. Bye!"
Grace says.
"Be careful."
Virginia cautions.
Grace struts.
Moments later, Virginia is seated on her white Rocker with the Flyer in hand. She rocks as she ponders. Grabbing the remote she turns on the TV. After the commercial, Breaking News pops up on the lower thirds of the Television screen. The News Reporter is animated.
"Maam, are you the mother of one of the victims, identified as Megan Cantine? I should be talking with you. "
The News Reporter presses through the crowd.

SAUCE

"Caroline Beckles, Morristown Eyewitness News. Seems like another horror faux pas or blunder."
Sissey Cantine nods.
"Yes? First, it was Jason. Then it was Sidney Prescott, Freddy Krueger, and now...?
Your daughter is the one being hunted, right?"
Sissey Cantine is furious.
"We will keep you updated on this growing story."
The Breaking News ends and goes to a commercial.
Virginia cuts off the Television.
"It better not come around here."
She says and places the flyer on the dining table. Subsequently, she heads to the closet in the other room. Virginia opens the closet. A large heavy-duty pitchfork FALLS out. Virginia coincidentally avoids a collision with the falling pitchfork. She picks up the tool, returns to her Rocker with the fork, and personalizes it.
"Four sharp teeth and one long handle. Uh-huh! I'll fork you like I am getting ready to plant tomatoes."
Through the small curtained window behind her back, the whistling wind blows. She can see the street.
Trash items and debris from the street take flight. She quickly closes the window and returns to her rocker. She rocks, poised.
James, her grandson at least 9 in age, awakened by the high winds, comes out from the bedroom rubbing his eyes.
"Grandma, what just happened? Why are we being tossed in a whirlwind? I am scared."

SAUCE

"James, did you say your prayers?"
Virginia asks.
"No, Grandma. I forgot."
James replies.
"Say your prayers because it is more than a whirlwind. The Devil in hell is coming."
Virginia, commands.
"Why do you have the pitchfork in your hand, Grandma? Wouldn't he just bypass our house, like in the plagues back in the days of Pharaoh? That's what Pastor said."
James states.
Virginia ponders.
"Bye Grandma."
James says.
Virginia kisses James on the forehead. James saunters back to his room.
Virginia heads to her clothes closet and dresses in denim coveralls. She looks herself over in the full-length mirror. Satisfied, she takes up the pitchfork and continues personalizing it.
"Just in case It thinks farming is a joke...let It come by. This is not a hay-day, fool!"
Suddenly, there's a knock on the front door. Virginia answers, pitchfork in hand.
The Masked Form wrestles Virginia to the ground. It grabs the fork and penetrates the head through Virginia's stomach.
Blood gushes out.

SAUCE

Virginia screams, groans, and stops breathing.
Moments later, the front door opens, and Grace, half-soaked from the rain, enters.
"Mom, it's me!"
Grace closes the door behind her.
"The weatherman never said it was going to rain. Everything in the news these days has to do with: It's coming to a place near you. Now it is pouring down. Need to grab my darn umbrella."
Grace says.
Ambling toward the living room, she notices the closet door half-opened.
Her curiosity peaks.
"Mom, why do you have the closet door opened, unattended?"
There's no answer.
Grace pursues.
"Mom?"
She utters underneath her breath:
"Must be sleeping."
Grace pushes the closet door to gain access to the living room. She sees her mother bloodied and lifeless with the pitchfork's head immersed into her body and its handle standing tall.
She screams.
The closet's door hinges creek as it widens back toward her.

SAUCE

With her back previously turned, she subsequently turns to face the closet's entrance. The Masked Form faces Grace with his dagger hoisted above her.
She screams.
SWISH! SWISH! SWISH!
Three stabs with his dagger penetrate her body.
She groans and collapses.
The Masked Form disappears with the dagger in hand.
James rushes out, nightmarish.
"Grandma, do you really want me to pray for...?"
He screams.
Terrified, James sees the fork immersed into Grandma's stomach, his mother lying next to her, lifeless, and blood draining from both.
James, screams louder than before.
He opens the window.
"Help! Please, somebody, help!"
His plea returns as an echo.
No one responds.
He flees to his bedroom. Grabs his pillow. Squeezes it tightly, James says:
"I am sorry, Grandma. Mom, I am sorry. I should have prayed. Prayer changes things. However, the Devil cannot prevail. I'll see you both up in Heaven."

SAUCE

10

B ack on the college grounds, Sissey Cantine pushes her way through the animated pool of Reporters and those assembled cops. Saddened, but Sissey is all business, with a rosary around her neck. The cross, not only pops but bling.
"Miss. Cantine..."
Greets, Sheriff Chase.
Miss Cantine eyes Sheriff Chase's tattered bloody

SAUCE

badge and uniform. One can tell by that stare and its post-stare she's an adversary of law enforcement.
"Don't Miss, me! Sheriff Chase? Cops? The killing of Emmett Till, The Rodney King beating, The beating of John Lewis. Do you know? The Usual suspects? Why did they put you on this job?"
States Sissey Cantine.
"I am one of the best, Miss Cantine. Plus, renowned for my longevity."
Says Chase.
"Really?"
Asks, Sissey Cantine.
Chase responds.
"No stranger to bloodshed. Plus, a motive is always connected to someone or something in the past or present. I have seen it all."
"Sorry, I live in the present and the future. Don't have an affinity with bygones."
Responds Sissey Cantine.
There is loud Radio chatter.
Another Sheriff officer AL RICE, Asian in his 40s, marshals his way amid the butchery remains. A protégé of Thomas Chase he goes to work right away. Putting his organizational skills to work, he quickly engages himself in capturing photo exhibits of the dead and the injured.
Other Sheriffs arrive and employ in sealing off this expansive crime scene. Dropping additional yards of

SAUCE

yellow crime-scene tape onto the compound, they buddy-up with Rice.

"Leap Year? Too long a February. Around this time everything goes helter-skelter, even the full moon does double duty. Excessive Babies get made..."

In that group of Sheriffs, there is a cop with a child. She nods "Yes" holding her stomach with both hands grouped. Chase senses that Rice needs to say less and finish the task at hand speedily. He looks across in his partner Al Rice's direction proposing a muzzling look. Rice gets it and dives in.

"Any suspects? Again, I ask are there any suspects in addition to The Masked Form, who assumingly is still at large?"

Meanwhile, onlookers press. Some engage in capturing footage on their cell phones. Some VENT. Some are SILENCED. Others trespass attempting to enter the sealed-off crime scene.

Tension mounts. Onlookers thin out accompanied by loud chatter.

An onlooker hinged on departing, lingers and vents.

"Is It still on the run? Parents get your kids home before dark. I am not going to get caught up in Its return. Did you see the eyes on that creature?"

Al Rice interjects.

"If you see something, say something!"

Sissey Cantine eavesdrops and lightens up over the usage of that progressive S – word. Before Thomas

SAUCE

Chase could get a word into this escalating Whodunit pow-wow. Sissey Cantine interjects,
"Megan is doing fine and in stable condition. That dagger penetrated close to her heart. It missed... What a relief?"
Staring at Chase, she continues,
"Everyone is a suspect until we find out who is playing this bloody game."
"A game?"
Asks Chase with surprise.
The News Reporter listening in, responds: "Unbelievable! Is that what we are hearing? This is now viewed as some sort of a...?"
Chase replies,
"I don't like games. People always tend to get hurt. Sometimes people die. Halloween Kills was a game. So was Scream, Saw, Friday the 13th, and the infamous Texas Chain Saw Massacre."
In Sheriff Chase's point of view: The killer is still at large and recently killed scores of new victims.
Chase digs in, busily capturing stills of the horrific crime scene.
Chase is focused.
A Sheriff officer collects abandoned scary masks as well as other discarded items, loads them into a cruiser.
There is quiet chatter as onlookers in a huddle close by pow-wows. They eye Sheriff Thomas Chase with suspicion. Could he be a suspect?

SAUCE

"Plus! Plus! Plus...? A plethora!"

Continues Sheriff Chase regarding the horror film genre.

Meanwhile, loud chatter arises as News Reporters oil their equipment for residual coverage.

Onlookers press. They want to cover the story based on their POV. Cell phones are positioned to capture LIVE video. On-the-beat Sheriff officers keep onlookers at bay. The clicking of pens prequel the readiness of Journalists collecting data.

Indistinct dispatch radio chatter transmits.

Sheriff Chase and Al Rice board a cruiser.

Tires squeal.

The cruiser motors off speedily.

Across town, a Drone soars over rooftops of homes and industrial buildings.

Moments later, on a surveyed side street at a local Bar, Sheriffs Al Rice, and Thomas Chase arrest mask-less Frank Castillo, mid-30s. They handcuffed him, hands and feet, and force him inside a cruiser with a reinforced mesh partition.

Doors slam.

Engine starts.

The cruiser ROARS away.

SAUCE

11

Exactly one-day sequencing the 4th anniversary of that horrific attack by The Masked Form on the Morristown College, Sheriff Chase rummages through a stack of the Crime scene still photos. One could hear loud paper crushing as he cans the stills during the process.

"No wonder Frank Castillo got released. No one saw him do it. I agree with the decision. Unmatched DNA? Nothing to see here!"

He grabs a cup of coffee.

SAUCE

Moments later, the door hinges creak followed in tow by footsteps. In walks Sissey Cantine. She is dressed in street clothes and displays an oversized Rosary necklace around her neck. The cross, bling. Thomas Chase reminisces. He remembers her as well as she does him. The greeting is mutual although seemingly somewhat distantly frigid.
"How is Megan?"
Chase asks cordially.
Sissey Cantine responds,
"The powers to be released their prime suspect? Frank Castillo, what a sleaze bag? Megan is a sure survivor...A chip off my block."
She pauses and continues,
"How about those other kids who perished in that College grounds melee."
Thomas Chase looks into the depths of Sissey Cantine's soul. Her crucifix blinks back at him.
His pit-bull response looms, and he bucks up.
"How may I help you?"
He asks.
"You haven't yet closed the case, Sheriff? You cannot, and you shouldn't. Many more will suffer the Devil's wrath. All it takes for evil to prosper is for one good man to fold his tent. The record states: His DNA doesn't match."
Sissey Cantine inquires.
"That's what they say. I don't believe it. That name. That name. That name bothers me."

SAUCE

Sissey continues.

Miss Cantine, did it ever occur to you that these probabilities exist?

Asks Sheriff Chase.

Sissey Cantine desires more. She listens intently.

"Sometimes, surnames encounter situations that would affect their population and whereabouts? This whole thing could have been a setup to terrorize the lives of you and Megan. The perpetrator could have killed her during that elongated terrifying ordeal. But didn't."

Says Sheriff Chase.

At this point, Sissey is reading Thomas Chase like a book. Meanwhile, Sheriff Chase is sweating beads of perspiration and awaiting the blowback.

Tension mounts.

Sissey Cantine eyes Sheriff Chase with penetrating eyes.

"*It wasn't me.* It is the system."

Says Sheriff Chase.

"That's what Shaggy said. You folded, Chase? You folded like a barbeque tent. A gentle breeze is all it took."

"The case against Frank Castillo has no teeth. Consider it water under the bridge. Plus, these creepy-crawly happenings always turn out to be figments of the imagination. It's amazing what one's thoughts could lead one to. Believe - if they believe it. It just might happen."

SAUCE

Chase states.
The door hinges creak, followed by footsteps.
Sheriff Al Rice enters uninvitingly and closes the door behind him.
"Officer Chase, pardon me. Didn't know you had a company of our past. Howdy, Sissey Cantine."
Al Rice says.
Sissey Cantine genuflects to Al Rice.
"My regards to you and your daughter Megan. How are you holding up?"
Asks Rice.
"Holding up? In less than 24 hours it will be four darn years since that brutal attack on Megan and others at Morristown College. Yet justice has not prevailed. It is all nothing but a Hoax."
Eyeing both Sheriffs, Sissey Cantine clutches her crucifix tightly. A tear trickles down her eye. She personalizes the cross and walks out with hurried footsteps. She boards her black pickup truck and slams the door. Tires squeal as her vehicle motors off.
With Sissey Cantine now out of their space, both Sheriffs stare watchfully at each other. Their eyes interlock.
Al Rice breaks the silence.
"The case is closed, right?. We have not ruled out Sissey Cantine as a possibility...?"
"Off the record! Do you think she just surfaced as our new target?"
States Sheriff Chase.

SAUCE

"Don't look it. However, she has never recorded a marriage, only two births.
Responds Al Rice.
"Could the absenteeism of those two male figures be enough probable cause to make them the prime suspects?"
Pondering, Sheriff Chase reclines in his chair.

SAUCE

12

On the day of **02:29:20**, the sound of rustling knives reverberates from the kitchen. Through the hallway leading to the living room, Sissey Cantine is packing a weekender suitcase. Sissey is confused.
"Megan! Have you seen my necklace?"
Sissey asks.
The rustling of knives discontinues. Megan, wearing an apron ambles through that hallway from the kitchen toward the living room. She finds her mother

SAUCE

seated at the huge dining table pouring a glass of red wine. Sissey downs the drink.

"I have no idea why I am going on this weekend's retreat with all construction workers, who I don't care for or want to share my knowledge and wisdom with any longer."

Says Sissey.

"Mom, sounds like you're courting a career change?"

Sissey Cantine gets up, paces, and views her luggage.

"Don't push me. I am so darn close to the edge."

Megan is silent, looking at the window curtain being swayed by the wind.

"So, you have not seen my necklace?"

Sissey continues.

"No, mom. You wore it yesterday, remember? Could you have pre-packed it for the trip inside your luggage?"

Megan responds.

"I don't think so. I would have remembered."

Says Sissey.

"Yes. You are so great with details. No wonder they requested you to be their keynote speaker at the Construction Symposium."

Megan encourages.

"That's why I picked construction over gardening."

Sissey bolsters.

Sissey pours another glass of wine and downs it. She attempts another glass. That move frustrates the heck out of Megan.

SAUCE

"Mom, that's two for the road. Another glass is one too much in my opinion. Under the wheel?"
Megan gives her mom that candid look.
Sissey Cantine takes a pass. They embrace.
"Drive safely, mom. See you tomorrow."
Megan says.
"Thanks. I will be staying at the..."
Megan interrupts and finishes the sentence.
"Marriott."
With hurried footsteps, Sissey heads through the door hastily. The wind continually blows through the open window of the living room. Megan moves to the window and sees her mother drive off. Megan slams the window and bolts it. Megan, with a song on her lips, returns to the kitchen and shelving knives.

SAUCE

13

Moments later, Megan was still seated at the kitchen table and multi-tasks shelving knives while on her iPhone. She busily checks off names on her list.

"Hello, Bob. That's right. It starts at 8:00 PM. Yes! BYOB. I do not have Dave's number in my new phone contact list. Be sure to invite him. See Yah!"

Megan grabs an incoming call.

It's Sue, her BFF from college.

SAUCE

"Hi, Sue. It is going down tonight at my house. Yes, 8:00 PM. I have fired up the oven and put some drinks on chill. So, bring some spicy snacks and hot dudes."
Another call comes in. Tessa is on the call.
"Megan, Hi. It's Sue. Thanks for the invite. Would not have missed this for the world. I am good for some veggies and some cold cuts. Just spoke with Dave. He will be accompanying me to your shindig."
Megan responds jubilantly,
"Yes! This party is on! *So, tonight we'll party like it's 1999...*"

IN THE MEANTIME, *on the roadway,* Sissey Cantine sees the silhouettes of a soaring ax and a Shape or Form. They cross the street on a head-on collision course.
BLAM
They collide.
The Ax viscously penetrates the head of The Masked Form.
Sissey screams out.
"Frank!"
The Ax is lodged in The Form's head. Blood gushes out. It plasters the windshield of Sissey Cantine's vehicle.
Frantically, Sissey activates the windshield wipers.
SQUEAK! SQUEAK!
The wiper blades are deadlocked handling the removal of the gooey semi-dried plasma from the windshield.

SAUCE

Suddenly, the axed Form vanishes, and darkness veils. Sissey Cantine's vision becomes obscured. Sissey Cantine's pickup truck motors off the road and over an embankment. Multiple tall trees keep it hostage. Sissey is livid. She pounds her fist on the steering wheel.
"Shit! Shit! Shit!"
The hinges of the driver's door on her pickup truck squeak loudly. Sissey painfully manages to exit the vehicle. She reaches for her phone. The phone is dead. Sissey opines.
Moments later, Sissey opens the mini camper, retrieves her chainsaw, and begins cutting down the trees to clear a path. She's no novice using the chain saw.

SAUCE

14

Partiers begin to arrive. House dance music reverberates. The driveway fills up with a variety of high-end vehicles, as Millennials and Gen-Z assemble. There is much chatter and laughter.
The full moon lights up the night sky through the blowing trees. As the wind blows, crickets chirp. At the front entrance to the house, acquaintances mingle and buddy up. The music echoes over Megan's soothing voice.

SAUCE

"Welcome! Glad to see you. Thanks for coming. Welcome! Glad to see you. Thanks for coming! Sam, you made it! I like those glasses."
SAM HASTINGS, Caucasian, with a Crew Cut, and in the mid-20s, he flames.
"Thanks. You do?"
Megan responds,
"Yep. Nerdy..."
"Can't wait for the Cha Cha Cha."
Sam says as he ambles inside.
In a pixie haircut, SUE DAVIS, Asian ethnicity, cultured, and in her 20s saunters into Megan's space. So does TESSA, with a Bang haircut and mixed ethnicity, charismatic, and in her mid- 20s. There is loud chatter among the trio. They embrace. It seems more than a reunion of sorts.
"How is our past President?"
Megan asks of Sue.
Sue responds,
"Sorry about the friends we've lost on 2:29:16. Megan, if the clocks were to be rolled back, you would have most def become the next president of our student body. I so admire your bravery. You have put this so well together."
Megan feels flattered.
"There has never been or ever will be any jealous bones in me toward you."
Sue continued.

SAUCE

"Agreed. And her determination...? I've never seen any lack."
States Tessa.
Megan BLUSHES.
"Thanks. In that scenario, I would have no doubt been delighted to be your protégé, Sue. You would have had to promise me you would leave your line open to all my calls. But I am out of that league. Hasta la vista, Spikes!"
Megan chuckles.
"Could you see Spikes, draped in his black gown with gavel in hand as if he's on the Supreme Court Bench?"
Megan imitates Spikes:
"No Chads and Dimples. No, Stop the Steal. This is a democracy, not an ideology. Just count the Morristown College votes!"
The partiers chuckle at her Spikes' rendition. The alumni high-five each other. Morristown College students cheer loudly. Megan's high praises are validated.
The music echoes.
Megan commands,
"Guys, It is getting crowded inside. I hope everyone has on their dancing shoes. Let's party, like a P, an A, an R, a T, and a Y!
The Partiers respond,
"That's how we spell PARTY! PARTY!!!"
"We must! It's a PARTY!"
Says Sue and Tessa jointly.

SAUCE

They enter through the front door. Music BLASTS. Mingling is at an all-time high.
The doorbell rings.
Megan accommodates. More guests arrive strutting their latest attire. The guests enter. Inside, the party pulsates.

SAUCE

15

Suddenly the music stops. Megan Cantine has the bully pulpit directly in the mid-hallway. She surveys the room.

Bob Singh, mixed ethnicity, in his mid-20s is seated in the recliner off to the side, and Megan's left close to the hallway. In that hallway hangs two portraits. One of Megan competed in track and field where she finished strong. The other and close to Megan's is Jesse Owens in the qualifying round for the Berlin Olympics in 1936.

SAUCE

Bob admires the two achievers' comradery. Bob zings Megan.

Sue Davis mid-20s is seated on a barstool close to the drinks. She swivels' on that stool.

Dave Simmons in his early 20s is seated in the love seat with Tessa Barnes. A side lamp rests on the table next to them. Tessa Barnes is in her late 20s.

Sam Hastings, Caucasian, in his mid-20s - is seated on the piano bench facing the loveseat. He Laughs at every joke. CARVER BANKS, African American, in his late 20s is seated on the left end of the couch next to Brandy O'Neal.

BRANDY O'NEAL, African American, with a low shaved haircut and in her late 20s is seated on the couch next to Carver and Caslin.

CASLIN CHOW, Asian, with a layered hairstyle and in her mid-20s is seated on the couch joining Brandy as the other rose between two thorns.

JOSH KRAVITZ early 30s, Jewish wearing a Yamaka hat is seated on the right end of the couch next to Caslin. In front of the couch is a center table with a vase filled with dried sunflowers. A large bowl of popcorn sits next to the vase of sunflowers.

LIZ MENENDEZ late 20s, Latinx is seated at the dining room table in the background to the right of Drew Soprano.

DREW SOPRANO in his mid-20s is seated at the dining room table in the background. He's Italian and

SAUCE

MOB-looking with legs crossed defining leadership at the head seat.
MELINA DEZOUSA late 20s, Latinx is seated at the dining room table in the background to the left of Drew. She's directly underneath the grand chandelier.
Megan presides,
"Welcome! Welcome! And Welcome. So fricking glad you all came. Especially those graduates from Morristown C."
She surveys the room, taking in everyone.
"I'm so glad we can get together on this 4th anniversary, after enduring that horrific tragedy 4 years ago today. To my other peeps, thanks for the support.
Everyone responded so darn swiftly and promptly to my invite. I just love the impromptu spirit. Reminds me of my tenure as a Sprinter, when it was all or nothing. In other words: Play Big or go Home."
The Partiers applaud.
"Tonight my house is yours. Put items back where they belong. My mother lives here too, and...if you see something, say something. Too much to drink? Feel free to have a sleepover. Let's commemorate..."
Dave, adoring Megan's portrait on the wall:
"You are our hero, Megan! Girl you can run. You were the best at our college in track and field and you certainly used your skill to outrun that monstrous blood-sucker."
"Dave, thanks...thanks For standing in the gap."

SAUCE

Megan responds.
"We love you, Megan! Let's tear down the ceiling and push back the walls with music..."
Says Bob.
The music pops and the partiers celebrate, toast, and commemorate.

SAUCE

16

Suddenly...automobile alarms echo. Partiers rush out and remotely disarm their alarms. Then rush to their vehicles. Megan tarries at the entrance door of the house surveying the disarming process. A cat meows loudly as it stretches its way across the driveway. Megan is on edge, scared.

Bob arrives at her side. He cheers her up by holding and squeezing her hand gently. The meowing subsides.

SAUCE

Coincidentally, Megan's phone rings. She ambles away from Bob and answers.
"Megan...Megan, Megan are you alone?"
Asks the Man's Voice.
"Leave me alone! I am going to call the Sheriff."
"Trouble. Party at the Cantine's house. Over!"
The Man's Voice responds. The voice sounds familiar. Megan screams out and cozies up next to Bob. She WHIMPERS.
The party guests return from checking on their vehicles.
"Thanks, guys. If your car battery gets drained, please feel free to crash until the morning. I have unlimited AAA."
Sam Hastings chuckles. He adjusts his spectacles to portray a deeper nerdy look.
"I love it! Unlimited AAA!"
Says Sam.
Dance music intensifies and the partiers return to celebrating.

WAILING SIRENS ECHO in the distance. Moments later, Sheriffs Chase and Rice pull up and discover an abandoned car in the bushes. They get out and investigate.
Sheriff Chase is alarmed.
"This car is registered to Spikes from Morristown College."

SAUCE

Chase and Rice escalate their search of the vehicle. There is no Spikes.
All of a sudden, Rice yells.
"Chase we've got something. Look up!"
From a tree, the carnage of Spikes hangs. Blood drips from it.
"We have got to find answers, soon. Too much foul play and the night is still young."
Chase says.
Al Rice is mute.
Car doors slam.
Tires squeal.
The two Sheriff officers depart and moments later, they arrive at the Cantine's house. After surveying, Chase rings the doorbell.
Megan answers.
"We are officers Rice and Chase."
Chase says.
"I know who you are Sheriffs. My mother gave me the 411 on the release of Frank Castillo. We are having a party and do not want to be bothered."
Says Megan.
"We are not here to disrupt your event. We have been dispatched to your residence because of excessive horny disturbances in a predominantly residential neighborhood..."
Chase says.
There is loud chatter from inside the house.
Bob asks,

SAUCE

"Megan, do they have a warrant? Bastards!"
"Megan, tell them you have an event to cater to. If they want to take you in for questioning. We are all going with you to that pigsty."
Dave says.
"Where is your mother, Miss Cantine?"
Asks, Sheriff Rice.
"Mom is a grown woman. Away on business. Why?"
Megan replies.
"Was Spikes invited to your event?"
Rice asks.
Megan, more annoyed than before, "Officers, why all these leading questions? Spikes is not my boyfriend!"
Chuckles echo from inside the house.
"We discovered his vehicle in the ravine across the way and his mutilated body hanging from a tree at the scene. I ask you again, was he an invitee to this party? When have you last spoken with Spikes or seen him alive?"
Chase asks.
"Spikes was never invited and that was not done on purpose. Just logistics."
Says Megan.
"Have you seen anything unusual in the area? Any masked individual, etc...?"
Sheriff Chase presses.
"No. None at all."
Megan responds.

SAUCE

"Be sure to call us regarding any other strange occurrences."

Chase states.

Megan responds,

"Have a good night officers!"

17

Megan returns to the party shaken up and in tears. Her guests press and huddle to comfort her.

"Somebody killed Spikes and hung his body from a tree. What the Hell is going on?"

All of a sudden, teary eyes permeate the party. The Morristown College alumni are terrified. They huddle in desperation.

"What are we going to do?"

SAUCE

Asked Sue in a somber tone.
Megan attempts to go and investigate the goings-on. Sue signals her need to stay.
"I called mom. She did not even pick up."
Megan responds.
"Is that normal?"
Dave asks.
The sighing Megan responds,
"She is conducting a seminar tonight."
The Partiers, now all huddled together stare at Megan in concern. Megan garners a burst of energy and renewed enthusiasm.
"You know what? Turn up the darn music. Bring out the beers. Let's party till the sun comes up. Hip Hip!"
The partiers now recalibrated, respond:
"Horray!!!"
"That's the Megan we know. Go, girl..."
Says Sue in support.
The Partiers validate,
"We are not going to be intimidated. We are all in! We are all in! We are all in! Let's rock the house."
Amidst loud chatter, Megan serves additional drinks. They cheer loudly.
"Let's celebrate. I say ...Let's all escalate and commemorate tonight..."
Says Bob, rhyming as Old school R & B music reaches a crescendo. The Partiers indulge.

SAUCE

Bob whispers in Megan's ear. She reciprocates. He escorts Megan to the bedroom. Sam sensing that move, coughs awkwardly.

Other partiers toast to the decision orchestrated by Bob.

Inside the bedroom, Bob and Megan make out.

SAUCE

18

Later, Megan and Bob return from their rendezvous as partiers dance to "All Night Long." The party is at an all-time high. Megan surveys and notices the beer stack decreasing.
Sue catches on and tries to get Bob's attention.
Drew holds up an empty beer bottle.
Megan summons Bob.
"We are all out? Check downstairs. There's some beer inside that large freezer."

SAUCE

Bob departs, energized. With loud hurried footsteps, he descends the stairs. Bob, la la la *Pretty Woman*. Several stairs lead to the lower level. Bob maneuvers, despite losing some soberness.
Squeaky sounds emanate.
Bob holds his own.
He locates that giant-sized freezer. Bob opens the lid. The thing is loaded with cartons of beer.
Bob smiles.
He salivates.
"Let's celebrate...brate, brate, brate."
Bob chants.
He relieves the cooler of three cartons of beer. He stacks them on top of each other on the floor.
Oblivious to Bob, the sound of loud footsteps reverberates. Bob methodically transports the first two cartons upstairs one at a time. The partiers aggressively grab and enjoy cold beers. Dave pops a cork and "cheers" to Bob.
Bob reciprocates with a MACHO smile.
The Crowd yells.
"Go, Bob. Go, Bob! Go, Bob!"
Bob shuffles his feet and returns downstairs. Bob is confronted by a Masked Form.
They SPAR.
They WRESTLE.
Bob is outmatched.
The Masked Form strangles Bob.
Bob falls to the ground.

SAUCE

It opens the lid of the giant-sized freezer. It agilely lifts Bob and stuffs him inside. It stabs Bob with a dagger. Pulls the dagger out of Bob's chest and closes the icebox. The Form secures the cooler with a nearby lingering padlock. It places the extra carton of beer on top of the freezer and mops up the bloody residue. The Masked Form takes off.

SAUCE

19

Over the embankment, Sissey Cantine mops the sweat from her brow. She re-loads her chainsaw into the mini camper. Using a liquid stored inside that camper, she rids the windshield of its impediment. Satisfied, she opens the driver's door and buckles herself in.

Subsequently, Sissey turns on the ignition key. The pickup truck doesn't startup. Second TRY. It doesn't respond. THIRD try...the engine starts. The pickup truck motors up the embankment and onto the main road.

A Rest Stop sign headers in the distance and the pickup truck motors in that direction.

Moments later, brakes screech, and the pickup truck parks. Looking in the rearview mirror, Sissey Cantine notices her unkempt hair. She shakes her head. *No* to her looks she agrees. Sissey grabs the weekender off the passenger seat and exits for the restroom. She is purpose-driven.

Using a stall Sissey Cantine does a quick change of clothing. After which she fixes her hair in the mirror and gets ready to leave.

Creaking hinges from the adjacent stall grab her attention. Subsequently, the stall door closes. A man coughs followed by moaning sounds. Startled, Sissey bends over to take a look inside. Underneath she sees black sweats with red and black sneakers attired on the Form.

"Frank?"

Sissey inquires.

No answer.

Breathing heavily, Sissey grabs her weekender luggage and DARTS out of the restroom, terrified.

SAUCE

20

Panning, Sissey Cantine re-boards the vehicle and continues en route. She is upbeat having escaped what could have been... Turning on the radio, she serenades herself with multiple upbeat tracks. The song stops abruptly and the Newscaster, a local, chimes in:

"This is FM 95 in MORRISTOWN. I am John Shephard with some late-breaking News: Today marks the 4th anniversary of the Morristown College dilemma which left six people dead and several more injured. Plus, humiliated Dean Spikes."

Sissey Cantine is attuned. However, wished she wasn't the targeted listener.

"Less than an hour ago, two MORRISTOWN Sheriff officers Thomas Chase and Al Rice discovered the abandoned vehicle registered to Dean Spikes, and later his carnage hanging from the tree nearby.

Ironically, that crime scene is located less than 100 yards from the residence of Sissey and Megan Cantine."

The tires squeal and the pickup truck takes a swift U-Turn. Sissey Cantine is furious. The vehicle swerves right then left almost colliding with a semi-tractor. Sissey Cantine is shaken up.

The Newscaster continues his news segment.

"You would remember Frank Castillo the potential serial killer, charged with victimizing students at the Morristown College, including Megan Cantine, and was acquitted of those charges at least three years after the incident. Same guy? More to come on this unfolding story..."

Sissey Cantine is not only frustrated with the Newscaster but with the news, he just dropped as well as what she sees in the distance.

Up ahead. The traffic jam gridlocks for miles. It is like a parking lot. Sissey Cantine attempts calling on her

SAUCE

phone. The Phone does not power up. She abandons the device in her weekender.

Ahead. She sees an open side street. The Pickup truck motors to it. Brakes screech as it comes up on Wooden Sheriff barricades facilitating the alternate flow of traffic. Sissey gets out of the pickup truck. Taking the situation into her own hands. Sissey Cantine grabs her chainsaw and nullifies the barricades.

Al Rice, Morristown's Sheriff on duty jumps out of his vehicle and confronts Sissey. Radio chatter transmits.

"Do you have any idea as to what the heck you are doing...?"

Sissey is livid.

They square off.

21

Back at the Cantine's residence, the party is Rokus. Megan dances semi-au naturel to her audience. Dave applauds and grabs a beer and heads downstairs. He is focused. He is mission-bound. Dave takes a swig of the beer. It is refreshing.

"Bob, where the heck are you? Buddy, you are missing out on all the fun. Megan is putting on a show of her life!"

SAUCE

Dave's footsteps escalate. He almost misses his footing. Balancing the beer he rebounds.
"Listen, we've gotten enough beers. Thanks. Greatly appreciated."
Dave sees the box of beers on top of the large freezer. And ambles in its direction. David touches the box. Lifts it. Oblivious to him, the freezer shook. He returns the box of beer carefully to its original spot.
"Oh, you've set up a box of reserves? Way to roll. It is your night."
Dave chuckles to himself.
"Have it your way, Buddy. But where the hell are you, man? Megan seems to be having such a good time. But underneath her disguise, she looks scorned. You know that's a bad thing to do to a woman? Psychologically they hold the offender hostage. Why?"
He takes another swig of beer.
"You make them feel like they have been prostituted."
Dave hears weird noises.
"Sorry, Man. I saw in you a friend, a mentor. Never knew that was part of your character makeup. You have deserted us! Abandoned the party!"
Ahead. Dave sees a half-open door. His face lights up. Purpose renewed. He moves towards it gracefully. A flashlight above the door gets his attention. He grabs it and peers out searching.
"Look, we all are grown men, right?. However, if you really wanted to take a piss...There are five full bathrooms upstairs, one for each room in this gigantic

SAUCE

house. Plus, half on the first floor for guests. You could have used anyone."

Dave discards the empty beer bottle in the nearby trash can.

"You dissed us! Have you crossed the fricking line? Hell YES! Dude, in the realm of friendship. We have been buddies since elementary. We have double-dated. We have hiked together…"

Mysterious sounds echo.

The wind whistles.

It rains hard. Dave savors the element and navigates the parked cars.

"I should have given you a ride, instead. But wanting you to impress Megan so badly, I insisted you DYOC. Now you FUB."

Dave searches for and accidentally stumbles upon Bob's BMW.

"Oh, there you are. I see it but I don't see you. Stop playing games, Bob Singh."

The two front doors are opened of their own accord.

"Darn, this automobile came loaded to the max. A Friend holding out on a friend, huh?"

Mysterious sounds intensify.

Dave is RATTLED. Scared. He resorts to back-stepping away from the BMW.

"That's not how this should be. Not how this should end. You've set me up, friend."

SAUCE

Moving briskly in Dave's direction is the bloodied Sheriff officer, Al Rice. The Sheriff uses his right hand to hold up what's left of his shooting hand together.
"How may I help you, Dave Simmons?"
Dave is appalled to hear a cop call him by his full name.
"Looking for my friend Bob. Have you seen him?"
Dave, states.
"Yes. I know where he is. Follow me!"
Dave refuses to comply. The flashlight still in Dave's hand goes out.
"Dave Fitz Simmons, you are refusing to obey the law. Jails are full because of offenders like you."
Says, Rice.
With one hand, Al Rice retrieves a set of handcuffs from his belt. Dave takes off hastily and bangs into multiple parked cars. His head penetrates a car's windshield.
Al Rice chuckles and travels on.

SAUCE

22

Back at the Cantine's house, Megan finishes her dancing performance and acknowledges a tumultuous standing ovation. Tessa, jealous of Megan's performance, whines. She grabs a beer. Pops the cork and takes a swig.
"Gosh! I've got to get me some air."
She heads downstairs.
"Dave, where did you go?"
There's no response.
"Dave, I do great lap dances... very, very freaky."

SAUCE

No one answers.

"Dave, we are almost out of beers. I grabbed the last one. Dah! What's up with you and Bob? Are you guys partners, bipolar?"

Tessa, states.

Ahead. Tessa sees a closed door and begins to pry it open. It does not budge.

"Don't worry guys. What happens at the Cantine's, stays at the Cantine's."

She releases her hold on the doorknob. The door opens of its own accord. Tessa's appalled, SCARED.

"Thanks, guys! Time out! This hide and seek is over."

A black cat strolls as it meows adding more fuel to Tessa's burning fear.

Tessa is terrified. She shivers. Sparsely. Large freezers fastened with giant-sized padlocks decorate.

Tessa is hesitant but prowls.

She sees human skulls, large Craniums, Mandibles, Maxilla, Clavicles and Scapula, Radius, Ulnas, Carpals, Metacarpals, Phalanges, Sternums, Ribs, Spines, Pelvic girdles, Femurs, Tibias, Fibulas, Talus, Calcaneus, Tarsals, Metatarsals, and Phalanges.

Tessa screams out.

"Boneyard in a basement? Murder! Murder! Murder!"

Hinges creak.

BLAM!

The door behind her recloses of its own accord. She feels trapped.

SAUCE

Tessa grabs the doorknob and tugs on the door. It doesn't budge. Tessa is frantic.

Tessa nursing her fear, screams.

In haste, she sees the garage door leading to the outside. She tugs HARD on it. She bangs on it unrelentingly. It doesn't budge. Tessa kicks the door out. It becomes unhinged. She sails through the open door and to the outside. She FALLS to the pavement. Gets up. Falls again. Gets up. She screams. She darts through the driveway and parked cars, screaming.

Strange sounds accompany.

She hustles.

The moon shows its fullness.

Peripherally. Sheriff Al Rice moves swiftly on her trail. Her speed is no match for him. Rice is slowed holding his semi-dislodged shooting arm in place with his right hand.

"Welcome to the real party! Where evil reigns."

Says, Al Rice.

"I can't stand cops. They terrify me. Rice, you helped acquit Frank Castillo. You're just a bunch of lying bastards! Are you the real killer?"

Tessa responds.

Tessa jets out of his space.

Al Rice catches up with Tessa as she stumbles. They wrestle. She's bloodied. He beats her severely with his baton.

Tessa yells,

"Rape!"

SAUCE

Rice backs off.
Tessa kicks him in the groin.
He WINCHES.
He falls to the ground.
Tessa takes off speedily. She U-turns toward the house in desperation, screaming.
Moments later, Tessa slams into Bob's BMW accidentally.
"Bob, what happened? What the hell happened, dog?"
A Man's voice sounds like Dave's…
"I have been waiting for you, Tessa. Bob is on his way."
Tessa sees the Silhouette disappear.
Tessa accelerates. Her path becomes vehicle-free and tree-friendly. The moon remains her constant companion.
She hears a loud sound of activated chain saws.
Tessa HUSTLES.
She SCREAMS.
She sees another silhouette. This time that of Dean Spikes, dressed in a sports blazer.
Tessa reflects,
"Dean Spikes, how did you know I was at the party? Remember that College dance? I've told you already that I have a darn boyfriend. You wouldn't listen."
Tessa insinuates,
"Take your… hands off me! You pervert…"
She JETS.
Ahead. Spikes' abandoned vehicle is in view.
Tessa SCREAMS.

SAUCE

Spikes' carnage falls from the tree and lands in front of Tessa. A rescue rope attached to the tree dangles.
"OMG!"
She SCREAMS.
Coincidentally, Tessa TRIPS and COLLAPSES crossways on top of Spikes' remains.

SAUCE

23

At the party, Megan picks on food from the food platter. She reviews the room.
"Where is everybody else?" Megan asks.
Sue gives her the "I don't know - look."
Megan insinuates,
"Gone to smoke?"
Sue responds,
"I didn't know Bob smokes."

SAUCE

Megan chuckles and replies:
"What happens at the Cantine's stays at the Cantine's, remember?"

ALONG THE ROADWAY, an aerial view shows Sissey Cantine's pickup truck speedily navigating traffic, erratically at times. The pickup truck motors to the left lane and speeds up. Vehicles being tailed give the right of way to the emergency vehicle. Sirens wail as the Sheriff cruiser in tow bears down with flashing lights.
Vehicles give way.
The Sheriff's cruiser gains on the black pickup truck. Brakes screech as the Cruiser tailgates.
Moments later, the pickup pulls off the busy road and onto a side street. The Sheriff's Cruiser pulls up behind the pickup truck and parks. Flashing cruiser lights illume. Other motorists eavesdrop.
Sheriff Chase steps out amidst loud radio chatter. He saunters to the driver's side of the black pickup truck. The driver's window rolls down. Chase peers inside the vehicle.
"Drivers license, insurance, and registration, please?"
Sheriff Chase, demands.
"Come on Chase, you know who I am."
Says Sissey Cantine.
"Drivers license, insurance, and registration, please?"
Chase asks.
"If you want it that badly, you can have them all."

SAUCE

Says Sissey Cantine handing over the documents.

"BTW, what is the charge Sheriff?"

Frowns Sissey Cantine.

"You were caught speeding erratically. My radar clocked you doing 120MPH in a 55MPH zone. That is considered reckless driving."

Says Chase, caressing his gun holster.

"Sheriff, your equipment malfunctioned."

Sheriff Chase responds,

"Tell that to the judge."

Sissey Cantine attempts to exit the vehicle. With his gun pointed at Sissey, Chase says:

"Wait inside the vehicle."

Chase returns to his cruiser. There is loud dispatch noise.

"Ten-Four."

Thomas Chase says.

Moments later, Chase returns to the pickup truck. He leans in.

"Where's my ticket, Sheriff?"

Sissey Cantine asks.

"Ticket?"

Asks, Sheriff Chase.

"Citation!"

States Sissey Cantine.

"Miss Cantine, I am going to have to search your vehicle."

"Why? The speedometer is in the dash."

Responds Sissey Cantine.

SAUCE

Chase looks at the weekender on the passenger seat. He notices bloodstains.

"What's in the luggage?"

Sheriff Chase, asks.

Sissey Cantine reaches for the luggage.

"Please don't. Put both hands on top of the dashboard. I've got this."

Sheriff Chase demands.

Satisfied, he moves to the passenger door, opens it, and searches through the luggage. Sissey Cantine's blood-stained clothing alarms him.

"It looks like you went hunting. No roadkill? Place your hands on the steering wheel, Miss Cantine."

Chase says and eyes Sissey Cantine with his gun pointed at her.

"Where are you heading to?"

"My home."

"Your home? Don't you live on the southern side of town? Shouldn't you be heading in the opposite direction? How did blood get on your clothing and luggage?"

Chase asks.

"Accident."

Says Sissey Cantine.

"What's inside of that mini-camper in the rear?"

Asks Chase.

Sissey pushes the door HARD. It slams Sheriff Chase and lands him on his back. Chase struggles to get up and does. Sissey Cantine exits in confrontation. Chase

SAUCE

shoots relentlessly at Sissey Cantine. She ducks out of the bullets. Click! Click! Sheriff Chase's gun is empty. They spar. Chase places Sissey Cantine in a chokehold. A car with extensive beaming headlights pulls up focusing excessively on Chase. The glare is too much for the Sheriff. He turns away covering his eyes with his hand.

Sissey Cantine outwits him, breaks loose, and re-boards her pickup truck. Tires screech and it motors off.

We see The Form under the wheel. The car vanishes, leaving Chase in its dust.

SAUCE

24

Back at the house, Sue returns upstairs exhausted after such a taxing adventure and not finding the rest of the team.
She exclaims,
"There's nobody downstairs."
Megan responds, briskly,
"Maybe they went to the car..."
"Which one? Whose?"
Sue asks.
Sam, who has been laughing at every joke all night

SAUCE

long coughs like he just choked from smoking a joint. He laughs at his joke.
"That sounds like the million-dollar question of the night. That's what smokers do. Smoking is more meaningful when done in an intimate setting."
Sam says.
Sue heads down the stairs again, exclaiming:
"I'm going to find those bastards."
"Tell them the party needs them, and some more beer."
Says Megan.
"I will!"
Sue replies.
Sue is focused but travels downstairs cautiously.
"Where is the darn beer?"
Sue sees the beer carton on top of the giant freezer. She lifts it.
"Great. At least I don't have to go digging for a brew."
Weird sounds echo.
Sue puts the carton back exactly where she found it. She threads softly.
"Don't worry about a thing,
cause every little thing gonna be all right.
Singin: don't worry about a thing,
cause every little thing gonna be all right!
Rise up this mornin,
Smiled with the risin sun,
Three little birds
Pitch by my doorstep
Singin sweet songs

SAUCE

Of melodies pure and true,
Sayin, (this is my message to you-ou-ou:)"
The Song echoes in a Man's voice. Sue Davis is attuned.
"Don't worry about a thing,
cause every little thing gonna be all right.
Singin: don't worry about a thing,
cause every little thing gonna be all right!
Rise up this mornin,
Smiled with the risin sun,
Three little birds
Pitch by my doorstep
Singin sweet songs
Of melodies pure and true,
Sayin, (this is my message to you-ou-ou:)"
"Bob is that you? Your last name isn't Marley. But you sure sound great. If this was your original, you'll most def be a Grammy contender."
There's a clanging sound. Sue shivers in her skin.
"I heard you but I can't see you. I'm not good at hiding and seeking. Unless I am always the chaser. Chasing brings out the bitch in me. Do you understand?"
Sue says as she shudders.
"Was that clanging sound meant to scare me or did you guys give up?"
Asks Sue.
Sue sees a closed-door ahead. She moves towards it. She grabs the knob and swings it wide open. Bed pillows fall out and cascade through a massive trap

SAUCE

door. In the meantime, loud footsteps echo in the background.

Sue looks back in the direction of the sound effects. Sue screams. The Masked Form tailgates with a hoisted dagger in hand.

Through the trap door, Sue sees not only fallen bed pillows but a school of venomous snakes along with human remains. Sue looks across to the other side but wouldn't dare cross over.

The Masked Form gains on her.

She screams, staring at the carnage and the serpents below. Peripherally, she sees the dagger about to penetrate her backside. Sue catapults herself to the other side of the trap door. Having landed on her side, she gets up quickly and hustles.

Sue progresses toward another door. She opens it. A pitchfork falls out almost striking her.

Sue is shaken up. She screams.

"Why the heck, are you guys putting me through this? How about a straight-up invitation to smoke? I need to right this minute. Please save me from this darn monster."

Sue asks as she comes up to another door. She turns the knob. It doesn't budge. That frustrates her.

"Oh, that's where you guys are? I need help!"

Automatically, the door opens up. Sue is relieved.

"Thanks! Private party?"

Sue enters the room.

SAUCE

An assortment of giant-sized human bones linger. She screams amidst clankings and chain saw cranks. Sue runs for cover. Meanwhile, the Chain Saw sounds crescendo. Looking over her shoulder, The Masked Form pursues her. Chain Saw in hand. Sue throws electrical fans, desk lamps, shelves, and other items in Its path. It wouldn't let up. Her heart pounds. Sue burst through the glass portion of the garage door. The Masked Form is slowed cutting its way through with the Chain Saw.

25

Sue is still on the run. She escalates and runs into the bloodied-arm Sheriff, Al Rice. He tackles her to no avail. In the backdrop, The Masked Form cuts its way through the garage door. Sue has eluded The Form through the parked cars. She calculates.

"Eeny, Meeny, Miny, Moe. Bob rolled up in that fancy BMW. Where the hell is it?"

In the interim, The Masked Form veers off on a beaten path.

While Al Rice plays catchup with Sue.

SAUCE

Accidentally, Sue STUMBLES into Bob's BMW. She is discombobulated.
"Darn, no wonder Megan led him to the bedroom."
Sue, says.
She knocks on its front passenger window.
No response.
Sue kicks the tires.
The two front doors open as before.
Sue scoots inside. Seats herself underneath the driver's wheel. The car doors, close of their own accord. There is something on the floormat. Sue double looks and investigates. It's a Gucci pouch.
She grabs the pouch and quickly opens it. Stacks of $100 bills fall out into her lap. Sue takes a wad of the cash and forces it inside her Bra. She smiles.
From Sue's point of view, the giant-sized freezer opens. Bob lies inside unmovable with a stabbed wound to his chest.
Sue screams,
"Murder!"
She DARTS out of Bob's car in haste and continues on the run.
Suddenly, Sheriff Al Rice gains on her.
She TURBOJETS.
Whistling sounds echo.
Sue stumbles into Spikes' carnage with Tessa's body lying crossways on top of his, symbolizing a bloody cross.
Sue screams.

SAUCE

Moments later, Sue recognizes Dave with his head penetrated through a car's windshield. His feet hanging down on its hood. He's lifeless.
Sue is discombobulated.
Again Sue screams.
She HUSTLES.
She GASPS.

SAUCE

26

Sue accidentally makes a B-line to the house and arrives still gasping for air. Her heartbeat rate climbs. It is pounding. Sue lands at the front door. After pounding it severely, the door opens. The Partiers flock accompanied by loud chatter.
"I thought it was that Sheriff again. You look bloodied. Were you out hunting? Where is the catch?"
Sam, questions.
"Look, that's not funny."

SAUCE

Sue, replies.

"Sorry, maybe I've had one beer too many. Now, I'll have to call Lyft or Uber."

Sam, replies.

Megan fumes. She intercepts the conversation and aids Sue inside. Entering the house Sue feels like she was previously starving for fresh air. She savors the indoors once again like it was her first experience on the inside. Subsequently, she challenges Megan.

"Megan, we've got to talk now."

"Oh, no! Oh, no!"

Vents, the Partiers.

Even so, Megan leads Sue to her bedroom.

Fear beams in their eyes.

"Sue, what's the suspense. I'm not your typical Alfred Hitchcock protege."

Megan, asks.

Sue unravels:

"Megan, I m your closest friend? Aren't I?"

"Yes. Of course. We met at Morristown College and bonded like crazy glue. You wanted the same things for me that you wanted for yourself. That, Sue, is true friendship."

Megan responds.

"Understood. This is more than a fricking mystery."

Sue recollects.

"You've never told me you live in a haunted house and that some of your friends are fricking dybbuks?"

"What are you talking about?"

SAUCE

Megan asks.
"There's a fricking boneyard downstairs. Filled with giant-sized human bones, everything from fingers to toes. Venomous snakes and human remains in your house? That is so darn grotesque. Plus, a Form with a mask trying to kill me."
Sue states earnestly.
"Sue, I think you are letting your imagination go wild. Were you smoking with the rest of the bunch?"
Says, Megan.
"I had nothing to smoke. Believe me or not. I'm telling you what I've seen. Bunch? They are all dead, Megan. Dead as tombstones."
Sue replies.
Megan sighs
"Sue, are you sure it was my house?"
"It is! Our best friend Tessa. Her body lies crossways on top of Dean Spikes, symbolizing a bloody cross. Since when did they decide to die together? They couldn't even live together for a few hours at that college dance, remember?"
Sue states.
Megan tears up.
"Dave's head is penetrated through a car's windshield."
Says, Sue.
Megan SCREAMS
"Oh, no. Poor Dave. Whose car was it? His?"
Megan asks.

SAUCE

"Yours. Your fricking car."

Sue replies.

Megan breaks down.

Moments later, Megan regains her presence of mind.

Sue continues,

"That Sheriff from the Morristown College incident..."

"Which one? There were two of them."

Says Megan.

"Al, Al Rice, the smart aleck. He was bloodied, using only one arm. Looks like somebody attacked him with a Chain Saw and disassembled his arm. Poor guy."

Sue replies.

"Oh no."

Megan says and proceeds to comfort the terrified, and bewildered Sue Davis.

"I don't understand. What the hell is going on? Every four years. At the same time?"

Sue lightens up a bit:

"They should make this a national holiday and call it 02:29."

Megan waits for the shoe to drop.

"...and Bob?"

Megan asks.

Sue responds,

"That's the mystery. I believe Bob is inside that giant-sized freezer, frozen to death."

"Do you know for sure?"

Megan asks.

SAUCE

"I visualized Bob lying there like a lamb to the slaughter. Kill me. What the heck, I just got laid. So you can kill me now."

Sue articulates.

Tension mounts between them.

"Sue, that my friend, is forbidden territory."

Says Megan.

Sue replies,

"My bad. Probably. That freezer is secured with a padlock. Why don't you go take a look?"

Sue states.

They scream.

"Who could have done this?"

Megan asks.

A moment of distrust weaves between them. After a brief pause, they embrace sobbingly. They dry their tears. With Megan taking the lead, they exit the bedroom in haste.

SAUCE

27

Dance music vibrates and Partiers boogie to the max. The invisible DJ scores.
Megan says to Sue:
"I've got this."
Megan grabs a flashlight and a bunch of keys. She storms downstairs. Sue waits at the top of the stairs, fearing to descend.
Megan hustles to that giant-sized freezer. She removes the carton of beer sitting on top and unlocks the padlock. Wanting to prove Sue Davis wrong, she lifts

SAUCE

the lid. To her amazement, Bob lies face-up bloodied and lifeless.
Megan screams:
"Murder!"
Megan gets ready to ascend the stairs. The stairs retract leaving an expansive gaping hole. Inside is a deep pit crafted with Punji sticks made of bamboo. Megan evaluates an ascent... The climb back upstairs seems treacherous and humanly impossible. Visually, she sees those spikes penetrating her body resulting in sudden death. The Masked Form prowls from the rear with a dagger in hand. Megan is trapped.
Megan SCREAMS.
She threatens:
"The penalty for trespassing in New Jersey is $10,000. Plus, possible jail time."
It pays her no mind.
Megan yells.
"Somebody call the police!"
To which The Form replies,
"They can't hear you. Even if they did, the Sheriffs wouldn't get here on time. They are overtaxed since I came to Morristown."
"Who gave you our codes?"
Asks Megan.
"Codes? I don't need codes. I am the past, the present, and the future...02:29. Before me, there was none other. After me, they all are playing catchup."
The Form responds.

SAUCE

All of a sudden, It fills her space.
Megan plants a kick.
They wrestle.
SWISH!
It stabs her with the dagger and bounces. The stairs extend back to their original state. Suddenly, loud footsteps echo as Sue rushes down the stairs. She sees the blood gushing from Megan's stomach. She briskly attends in tears. Megan bleeds through her back and stomach.
"Help!"
There's a LOUD COUGH.
Megan vomits up her mother's necklace.
Eyeing the crucifix, Sue is terrified.
Sue SCREAMS.
"What the hell is this? OMG. Did you swallow a Cross? A whole darn necklace?"
Sue asks.
Eerie sounds accompany.
The overhead lights sway. The wind gusts through the cut-out in the garage door. Items fall from shelves.

SAUCE

28

The Music stops. Hurried footsteps reverberate as the Partiers rush downstairs. They notice the bloody scene.
Sam SCREAMS:
"Who the fuck did this? Who is the sleazebag...?"
Surveying the other Partiers, Sam asks in macho gobbledygook:
"Which one of you is the Stabber?"
Sam continues.
No one responds.
"I've called the medics. She needs some air. Thanks!"

SAUCE

Partiers respect Sue's plea for privacy and head back upstairs. They chatter amongst themselves.
Moments later, Sue rushes back upstairs and exclaims: "The party is over guys. There have been a series of murders at the residence."
BRANDY O'NEAL, CARVER BANKS, CASLIN CHOW and JOSH KRAVITZ seated on the couch aren't happy with the news about leaving.
"What's up with that? Do you guys think we are the killers?"
"No one ever said you were."
Says Sue.
"Could it be that you are possibly alluding...?"
States Brandy.
"Where's the next party? This one sucks!"
Says Caslin.
"Josh, could we go to your house?"
Asks Brandy.
Josh glances across the room at Carver and looks him over. Josh smiles,
"I have some extra Yamaka hats in the car black, all sizes, handmade, 100% cotton."
Carver smiles and gives Josh "thumbs-up."
"Let's do it."
Says Josh.
They get up to leave.
Drew draws his gun at them.
"Sit back down!"
Partiers are terrified.

SAUCE

Drew continues,
"The killer always leaves first."
"The Killers."
Says Sam.
"Guys, let's not do this. I have seen enough bloodshed in one night."
Sue says.
Drew waves his gun. He draws it on Sue.
Melina DeZousa gets up from her seat.
"You guys are not leaving. I have not gone to the restroom all night. Call the cops."
"My dad will kill me if I get arrested tonight. I'm only…"
Says Carver Banks.
Drew removes pointing the gun at Sue. He aims it on Carver.
"So, it is you. You are the killer."
Drew alledges.
"Sorry, Guys. Grab your things and drive safely. Be careful."
Sue says.
"Sue, you are the fricking killer and now you are kicking us out. Where is Megan? She invited me and I am not leaving until the killer or killers have been identified."
Drew responds.
"Guys, I have been quiet since we were told we are being kicked out but I am not leaving until the killer fesses up."

SAUCE

Liz says.

Sue heads back downstairs.

"We have another party to attend. We are out of here." Says Carver Banks.

BANG! BANG! BANG! BANG!

Drew opened fire, killing Brandy, Carver, Caslin, and Josh.

In the aftermath, Sam asks:

"What did you do that to prove? Now you are the killer. We all have seen you kill them. Killer! Killer. Killer! Killer!"

Drew points his gun at Sam. Now the intended victim, Sam is warped.

CLICK! CLICK!

The gun is out of bullets.

Sam grabs Drew and wrestles him to the ground. He takes the gun and penetrates its BARREL through Drew Soprano's windpipe. Blood gushes out as from a spigot. Drew falls to the floor and struggles to his death.

Sam is relieved and poses a replica of the Mask in question.

29

At Morristown Hospital, Medics wheel the gurney in carrying Megan Cantine. Sheriff Thomas Chase accompanies wearing his grimy uniform. He is well angled so his bodycam consumes it all.

Loud radio chatter transmits.

One can see a teary-eyed Sue in the backdrop. She is terrified. She cries, and waves at Megan as the gurney rolls along.

SAUCE

Multiple Reporters have planted themselves outside. Megan is briskly transported on the gurney. Emergency staff and News Reporters crowd the process.
"We've got to keep it moving."
Says the Medic.
The Medic HUSTLES while patients and some medical staff give way.
The Gurney wheels squeal.
Later, Megan lies in the bed all hooked up with numerous tubes and cannula dispensing life support intravenously.
She ACHES.
The Nurse, a woman in her late 50s surveys, makes the sign of the cross and departs.

MEANWHILE, AT THE CANTINE'S HOUSE, the driveway has thinned out of vehicles. Sam is seated in his car. Headlights beam. He reflects. Suddenly, the headlights go out.
A Man's feet displaying red and black sneakers complemented with black sweat pants, struts across the front of the vehicle. The same gear was worn inside the restroom during the Morristown College Melee four years ago and earlier at the rest stop and the Cantine's residence.
The engine cuts off.
The suspect: The Masked Form ushers Sam out of the vehicle. Sam refuses and swings at It with a baseball

SAUCE

bat. He misses the hit. The bat sails multiple yards. The Masked Form grabs Sam by the neck with one hand. Sam's feet dangle. Using the other hand it gouges out both of Sam's eyes. The eyes fall to the ground and in a puddle of water. It releases Sam to a thunderous fall.
It DARTS on the driver's seat.
The door slams.
The engine starts.
The car roars away from the Cantine's residence.

SAUCE

30

Megan sits up in bed. Multiple life support tubes are attached to her body. The Nurse is seated across from Megan. The Nurse breaks the silence between them.
"So, somebody is trying to kill you? Do you know who and why?"
She, asks Megan.
Megan reminisces.
"No idea. I have not done ill to anyone to deserve this."

SAUCE

Megan responds.
"Where is your mother? Alive?"
Asks the Nurse.
"Yes. She's out of town on a business trip."
Megan responds.
"Boyfriend?"
Asks, the Nurse.
"My new guy? He was killed a few hours ago at the same party."
Says, Megan.
"Sounds like a Serial Killer for all I know. Most tend to kill until their stamina runs out. That's when they are most vulnerable to someone else's onslaught."
The Nurse says.
"Bob? Oh no. He is too cool of a guy to hurt someone. I call him my Teddy bear."
Says, Megan.
"Really?"
Asks, the Nurse.
"Are you saying I should never trust my love interest?"
Asks Megan.
"You need to learn one thing. In this world, everybody is a darn suspect."
Megan ponders.
"You call Jack a Jack and Spade a Spade, don't you?"
Megan asks.
"Where is your dad? Is he alive?"
"I have no idea."
Says Megan.

SAUCE

"Any siblings? Brother?"
Asks the Nurse.
"Not sure."
Megan says.
"Girl, you need to have some kind of epiphany about those who are stepping into your world and especially those who already exist in it."
Says the Nurse.
"So what are you saying?"
Asks Megan.
"I am not saying anything. It is none of my business. Not only do you look butchered but within the last 4 years, your name has been reported in the news all over Morristown in the same scenario. I am no shrink and I hope you are not recording this conversation."
The Nurse gets up and adjusts Megan's pillow to accommodate their eye level. She is satisfied. Returns to sit down.
There's indistinctive chatter.
She changes her mind about sitting down. Instead, she surveys the room as well as its surroundings. Still, on her feet, she looks Megan squarely in the eyes.
"Because if you are. I might have to kill you."
The Nurse shows Megan the DISPENSER.
Megan SHUDDERS.
"To be continued..."
Says the Nurse fixing to make her exit.
"Anything else on my brother?"
Megan asks.

SAUCE

"Anything else? That information is classified, redacted, on purpose."

The Nurse departs.

SAUCE

31

At the Cantine's residence, Sissey Cantine pulls up into the driveway and hastily enters her house after being gone for almost twelve hours.

Moments later, sirens wail. Subsequently, a Morristown Sheriff's vehicle pulls up and stops. Out steps Sheriff Chase. He rings the doorbell. Sissey Cantine answers. She is wearing that same necklace that her daughter vomited out.

SAUCE

Chase asks,

"Miss Cantine, long trip. Any explanation about this goings-on at your residence?"

"I have just returned. Will you give me a chance to breathe?"

Says Sissey Cantine.

"You can breathe on the way to the station. I am going to have to take you downtown and have you answer some questions."

Sheriff Chase answers as he puts handcuffs on Sissey Cantine. He pushes her inside his cruiser.

The doors slam.

The engine starts.

It motors off.

IN THE MEANTIME, on the other side of town at Morristown Hospital, Megan is resting. The Nurse enters the room. Megan jumps out of deep sleep. She opens her eyes.

"Thanks."

Says Megan with a smile.

"You are welcome. So you have been able to assimilate some of my world views?"

Megan answers,

"I have. Now I am wondering if I have a brother or if I'm living out the life of a fictional character in a Danielle Steel's novel."

"You do! I was one of the first to see the test tube specimen when I worked over at OBGYN, in addition

SAUCE

to Maude Collins our Head Nurse back then. She still heads up that department."
The Nurse says.
"You are fricking kidding me."
Megan replies.
"No one ever told you?"
The Nurse asks.
"This is news to me."
Megan responds.
"It was abandoned and given up for adoption. Because..."
Hearing such, Megan turns and aches. She interjects:
"Your characterization undervalues..."
Megan SIGHS.
"Really? It is what It is. You said I call a Jack a Jack and a Spade a Spade, didn't you?"
Megan aches.
She groans.
"Relax. Don't hurt yourself. Your wound needs plenty of time to heal. That cut went through and through. Someone wants your heart."
The Nurse chuckles and continues,
"You are very lucky to be alive."
The Nurse says.
Megan responds,
"I only have one life to live. Might as well know everything important to me before I cross over."
The Nurse asks,
"You are not leaving us now, are you?"

SAUCE

"There's a whole lot more I still need to know...Do I have a brother?"
Megan asks.
"You do."
Megan WHIMPERS.
"Really?"
Megan asks.
"Sorry if it cuts too deep."
Says the Nurse.
"My cuts can't get any deeper."
Megan says.
The Nurse shows her a baby pic from Google's photo collection on her iPhone.
"This pic is a replica of the original. You guys resemble each other. Same nose. Same eyes. Same lips. Except you are a much lighter complexion. Don't you think?"
Megan waits for the next shoe to drop.
"It was one of those first test-tube babies. The first was Louise Brown. She was born in London over 40 years ago. About exactly 4 years apart..."
The Nurse continued.
Megan asks.
"Four years, huh?"
"It was conceived outside of the human body through **IVT** (In-vitro fertilization). Its embryo was transferred from the jar "desiccator" and transferred into Sissey Cantine's womb. Nine months later It arrived. They called It Frank."
States, the Nurse.

SAUCE

Megan turns.
She aches.
She tears up.
She sighs.
"I told you it was going to be painful. Sorry."
The Nurse's phone rings. She answers.
"That's my old boss, Maude Collins on the phone."
The Nurse says to Megan.
"Jill, be careful what you say to that girl. It could come back to haunt us. We must let sleeping dogs lie. Remember, Blood is thicker than water..."
Says Maude Collins.
"You are so right, boss woman. See you at the party."
Says the Nurse. After which, she ponders.
"Tell me more. I was born to handle pain."
Megan says.
The Nurse dried her tears and watched as Megan's tears fall.
They recoup. The Nurse holds Megan's hand. She squeezes it tightly.
"Tell me more. I didn't come here to heal my physical wound. I came here to find out the plain... truth. Please."
The Nurse says,
"I understand."
"Which state is he in?"
Asks Megan.
"I am not sure if I can give you that information."
Megan waits in earnest.

SAUCE

"Off the record. Oh, I forgot you said you didn't want to die intravenously.
Megan SIGHS.
"Your mother abandoned It. Later It was given up for adoption."
Says the Nurse.
Megan SHUDDERS.
"When is Frank's Birthday?"
Megan asks.
"Split Persona? 02:29."
Says the Nurse.
"Where is Frank now?"
Megan asks.
"I do not want to get caught up in your family sauce. Your mother knows It like a poet! Ask her!"

32

Sissey Cantine detained at the Sheriff's Department Jail, presses up against the iron-gated door. She fumes in total disarray.
Loud footsteps echo as Sheriff Thomas Chase walks the hall. Sissey Cantine gets his attention.
"Sheriff, I need to make an urgent call to my daughter. Can you oblige?"
Chase shows little concern for Sissey. He looks at his watch.

SAUCE

"I'll let you know if we can accommodate."
Chase says.
Moments later, Chase confers with his Lieutenant, OSCAR CHILDS, a man in his senior years, frail and gray-haired. Childs chews Tobacco.
"On the outside, she has been a menace to us. Now she wants the world."
Childs says as he spits out...
He continues,
"No special privileges! None. Sissey Cantine has been a menace to our city."
Thomas Chase kowtows and continues on his beat.
Subsequently, Sissey Cantine is speaking on the landline phone:
"I would have visited you but that darn Sheriff, Thomas Chase has a vendetta against me and arrested me as soon as I got to our house. What happened at the house, Megan?"
Thomas Chase ambulates. He eavesdrops.
"At the last moment, some friends and I decided to commemorate 02:29:16."
Megan says.
"Why didn't you call me?"
Asks Sissey Cantine.
"Is something wrong with your phone? I tried calling you, multiple times."
Megan says.
"It is time for a new phone. Maybe I'll get an iPhone like yours."

SAUCE

Her Mom replies.
"How was the Conference?"
Asks Megan.
"Fender bender. Never made it. Good thing I took my Chain Saw with me to cut my way out of it."
States Sissey Cantine.
Thomas Chase strides again. He looks at his watch.
"They give you something in one hand and they take it back in the next. This was supposed to be a private call. I'm not sure they are going to let me out of here on bail."
Contends Sissey Cantine.
"Mom, you don't have a bad wrap."
"You are so right. I don't. Thanks."
Megan responds,
"Except..."
"Except what?"
Her Mom asks.
Megan responds,
"You fricking lied to me all these years, mom. Why didn't you tell me I had a brother and you gave his ass up for adoption?"
There's silence. No response.
Megan continues,
"Is his name Frank Cantine or Frank Castillo? Which one? How come you never showed me his baby picture? You can't be trusted, mom. I Wish you rot in there and go to hell."

SAUCE

"I can explain it all. Who fed you that information? I'll sue that darn hospital including that darn Hospital Director!"

Says, Sissey Cantine.

Megan hangs up.

Sissey Cantine tries to redial and gets a BUSY TONE.

Sheriff Chase ambulates.

"Time's up. Someone else is waiting to use that phone. Move it Cantine!"

SAUCE

33

On the College Grounds at Morristown College, Michelle Myers, the reporter from NEWS 8 warms up. Her Cameraman sitting inside the News Van is poised. Suddenly, she goes LIVE.

"I am Michelle Myers from News 8. We are standing in the same spot we did four years ago at Morristown College where six students were brutally murdered and several students injured including Megan Cantine.

SAUCE

Arrested, charged, and finally acquitted of those charges was Frank Castillo. The man, who we just learned today on the 4th anniversary of that college tragedy, goes by an alias, Frank Cantine."

She pauses and continues,

"According to sources, Frank is the son of Sissey Cantine and the late Joseph Crow. Also, he's the sister of Megan Cantine one of the injured victims in that college incident.

News 8 has also learned that Megan Cantine was brutally stabbed again tonight at their home and rushed to the hospital. She remains in critical condition. More to come on this breaking story."

This breaking news is watched not only by locals in Morristown but in bordering cities. Watchers as a result double-check their locks that night. Coincidentally, it was also viewed by the Nurse on a laptop in the medicine supply office.

THE NURSE IMMEDIATELY secures the room. She checks the locks thoroughly.

The Phone rings.

She ignores and quickly locates a liter Infusion Bag from the nearby overhead cupboard. From a generic shopping bag, she retrieves three small bottles.

The bottles read:

Pavulon
Potassium Chloride
Midazlam.

SAUCE

The Nurse pours equal portions of the fluids into the Infusion Bag. She puts it on the mobile tray and wheels it briskly to Megan's room.
She finds Megan asleep.
"Megan, it is your nurse, Jill Gordon."
There is no response from Megan.
The Nurse waits for a beat and then briskly trades out a 250 cc Infusion Bag marked SALINE for that NO NAME fully loaded One-liter Infusion Bag on the tray. She attaches it to the tube leading to the Cannular attached to the vein on Megan's arm.
Observing the Cannula, the Nurse states,
"Gauge 20. That's perfect."
She checks the flow from the Infusion bag. Drip! Drip! The stream is looming.
"Adios!"
Says the Nurse as she gets ready to bounce.
Megan tosses in bed.
The Masked Form barges in. The Nurse is startled. She is trapped. It closes and locks the door. It wrestles with the Nurse. It quickly subdues her. Fluid continually drips from the Infusion Bag into the tube leading to Megan's arm.
Its other giant-sized hand reaches over and removes the Cannula from a vein on Megan's wrist. The initial fluid dripped only on Megan's wrist. It stabs Cannula into a vein on the Nurse's arm.
"Ouch! Fuck you!"
Says the Nurse during the insertion.

SAUCE

The Form holds the Cannula in place on her arm. It squeezes on the infusion bag. Fluid begins dripping swiftly and flowing to the Cannula.

"You Uncircumcised maniac from the depths of hell. Your BO has not changed over 35 years. You still smell the same way you did. Rancid! Get yourself some chlorine bleach..."

Says the Nurse.

"Bitch. There are only two ways to die. Which do you prefer? Slowly or quickly?"

Says The Form.

The Nurse hits her knees. She mumbles with one hand raised heavenward. The Form plops her into her vacant chair. Peering into her eyes. It squeezes hard on the infusion bag multiple times, intensifying its flow.

"Don't fuck with the Health Department. What happens at OBGYN, stays at OBGYN!"

States The Form.

The Nurse COLLAPSES.

Suddenly, she stops breathing.

Megan turns and tries hugging The Form. It slips out of her attempted grasp and vanishes.

34

Megan energized and fully attired in street clothes emerges from her hospital room. Front line workers thin out.
They are terrified.
They SCREAM.
Megan SCUTTLES.
A sign ahead reads **OBS/GYN**.
Megan hustles and follows the arrow.
She lands at a door. The black and gold-lettered nameplate reads Maude Collins, Head Nurse.
Megan pushes the door HARD.

SAUCE

Maude Collins at her desk jumps up in surprise.

With a burst of energy, Megan grabs her by the throat. Raises her off the ground. Her legs dangle. Megan DROPS her to the ground. Using a pair of scissors off her desk, Megan gouges out both of Maude's eyes. She then STABS her in the stomach with the same pair of bloody scissors.

Megan struts to the Hospital Assistant Director's office. Adorned in horn-rimmed Spectacles, the Assistant Director in the late 50s sits at the desk shuffling papers.

Megan surveys. Megan looks through the glass on the wooden door. Megan barges in, unannounced.

"Don't you believe in knocking before entering? How may I help you?"

She says.

"Too many questions as an opener."

Megan replies.

The Hospital Assistant Director responds,

"Aren't you the girl...?"

"There you go again. Bitch you don't listen. How did you get this cushy job, nepotism? When I said ask no questions, that's what I mean."

Megan says.

Megan grabs the standing lamp in the corner. Hits it on the desk. That blow removes the shade and bulb. The Hospital Assistant Director jumps up out of her seat.

The Hospital Assistant Director, terrified claims:

SAUCE

"It wasn't me. The OBGYN makes its calls when it comes to...Ask me what you may. I have answers instead of questions."
"So, it was you. It was your greenlighting...?"
Megan asks.
The Hospital Assistant Director responds:
"We all had hunches we should abandon carrying out this insemination but to us, it seemed like performing a non-consensual abortion. Your mother wanted to have It."
"And you didn't inform her that she was impregnated with or by a Shadow, a Form, Why?"
Asks Megan.
The Hospital Assistant Director responds:
"I am afraid that information is classified. I cannot betray..."
Megan forces the lampstand through her stomach. Blood gushes out. She falls backward onto the floor and stops breathing.
Megan closes the door behind her and HUSTLES.
Around the bend, Megan sees a nametag pinned onto the shirt of a man of small stature. The nametag reads HOSPITAL DIRECTOR - Charles Baldwin.
He sees a patchwork of blood on Megan's clothing.
The Hospital Director states:
"Miss, the ER is down on the first floor. Not on the eleventh. You must have gotten your numbers mixed up."
"Now you are calling me F...dumb."

SAUCE

Megan responds.
"It is you...maybe not in body but physically and mentally connected to It."
He states.
"It is a given, that the root of the tree is connected to the trunk, the trunk to the branches, and the branches to the leaves."
Says Megan.
The Hospital Director responds:
"Those were your words.
Understand, your brother as part of a tree is connected to a killer, not only in the past but in the present."
"Delayed intelligence on your part for pouring orange juice into milk. That is nothing but some dumb-shit."
Megan responds.
Megan grabs him by the neck and twists hard. He groans as he falls to the ground.
Megan bounces.

SAUCE

35

At the Cantine's house, a News 8 Broadcast Van pulls up and parks. The engine cuts off followed by the slamming of doors. News Reporter Michelle Myers steps out. Microphone in one hand and pad in the next.
The Cameraman, already out of the vehicle preps for Broadcast.
Michelle Myers heads for the house. She rings the doorbell and waits. The door opens. She goes in.
On the TV monitor inside the van, Megan Cantine gives Michelle Myers a tour. Suddenly, the footage

SAUCE

stops. The monitor inside the van goes dark. The Cameraman troubleshoots to resume coverage. Nothing. Zip. He checks for audio. Nada. He takes off in haste toward the house, toting a boom mic. He opts not to ring the doorbell. He sees the door partially open. He ponders and eventually enters.
"Michelle, coming through. We need a reset. Encountered some technical problems, on the monitor; you went dark. How is your mic?"
Cameraman News 8 states.
No one answers.
He proceeds.
Drip, Drip, Drip, Drip - blood drips onto his microphone from up above.
He SCREAMS.
He stops.
He surveys.
The Cameraman looks up and sees Michelle Myers tied up with a rope by both feet. Bloodied with a dagger lodged from chest to back, and blood dripping out steadily.
Again he SCREAMS.
"Why did I get into this?"
He asks himself.
He back-pedals.
He turns around and winds up face to face with Megan Cantine.
SWISH! SWISH! SWISH!

SAUCE

A similar dagger lodged in his co-worker's body pierces through his chest and protruded through his back. Blood gushes from his multiple wounds.

Megan moves on.

He SCREAMS.

He MOANS.

He TUMBLES to the ground.

Moments later, a Sheriff's cruiser pulls up next to the News 8 van. Sheriff Chase and Al Rice jump out. Rice, still nursing that left arm now bandaged up, follows Sheriff Chase in tow.

They survey.

They notice the News 8 van is unoccupied.

They walk to the front door.

Chase rings the doorbell.

Megan answers.

Despite a dagger in hand, they aggressively tackle and take her down. Rice with the gun in his right-hand points it at Megan Cantine. While Chase does the takedown.

During the takedown, Megan asks,

"Where is your warrant?"

"Your biometrics are all over this city. You are going to need a darn good lawyer."

Chase says.

"We have been watching you for a long time, Megan Cantine."

Rice says.

SAUCE

The two Sheriff Officers escort Megan Cantine in handcuffs to their cruiser.
They jump in.
Slam doors.
The engine starts.
Sheriff Cruiser motors off.

SAUCE

36

Later, an Eyewitness News van pulls up outside the Cantine's house. The property remains sealed off with yellow tape. Reporter Caroline Beckles and her Cameraman step out. They engage in deep prep.

MEANWHILE, tired on this long night, Sheriff Chase walks into his house befuddled. He grabs a soda pop, removes his cap, and plops down on the living room couch. He turns on the TV. A cartoon commercial is rolling. All of a sudden, a clanking sound echoes.

SAUCE

Sheriff Chase DARTS to the kitchen in take-down style. There is nothing. He returns to the couch. The commercial ends.

"This is Eyewitness News. I am Caroline Beckles. We've got Breaking News."

She pauses.

"I'm standing outside the home of Sissey Cantine and her daughter Megan Cantine. As you would recall, Megan Cantine was the victim of a horrific chase and brutal stabbing by the alleged Frank Castillo at the Morristown College not too far from where I'm standing. Two students and four others also died in that incident. Frank Castillo was arrested, charged, and acquitted for those crimes."

She grabs her notes.

"Recently, according to sources but not yet confirmed by our network, we learned Frank Castillo also has an alias Frank Cantine and is the brother of Megan Cantine."

She pauses.

"Over the last few hours Megan Cantine, now the alleged flippant, has left her fingerprints on the killings of at least seven individuals including two reporters from our sister network News 8, 2 directors from Morristown Hospital, a Head Nurse, and others yet to be confirmed. Megan Cantine was arrested almost one hour ago."

Another pause.

SAUCE

"While, according to other sources, the Biological mother Sissey Cantine, has also been arrested for similar crimes. On the other hand, not much is known about the late Joseph Crow, except that while alive, he was known to have frequented cemeteries.
More to come on this Cantine family saucy chronicle. Remember, It could be on a street near you."
Thomas Chase is off the couch.
"It darn sure could! This monster is for real."
He rushes to the bathroom and washes his tired face. He puts his cap on. He turns off the TV and heads out the door in haste. Sheriff Thomas Chase hits the streets.
TIRES SCREECH.
His cruiser does a skid and recalibrates. The cruiser, gunshots through the streets of Morristown. He pulls up on a huddle of overalls-attired locals flagging him down in the solicitation of aid. Chase rolls down his window and bullhorns.
"Stop it before it stops us. More than a boogeyman. It is real, lethal, and dangerous. This may be the fight of your lives."
The cruiser picks up speed. Leaving those villagers wanting more.
That declaration echoed.
Crowds thin out.
Sheriff Chase persists.
The Form is nowhere in sight.

SAUCE

37

Across Town, The Masked Formed has just exited a grocery store. Inside, the dead owner was stabbed multiple times. A Sheriff's car pulls up.
BRAKES SCREECH.
DOOR SLAMS.
The Masked Form prowls.
A Sheriff dares the Masked Form.

SAUCE

Rifle pointed at It.
BANG, BANG, BANG, BANG, BANG.
Bullets rain on The Form.
It moves freely and unscathed.
CLICK! CLICK! CLICK! CLICK!
The Sheriff's rifle is out of bullets. No time to reload.
The Masked Form occupies his space.
The Sheriff resorts defensively to his baton and anything else in reach, still holding onto and pointing his rifle expectant of a magic bullet. Now, out of available defensive objects, the Sheriff back steps toward his cruiser.
The Masked Form pursues and confronts the Sheriff. The officer falls and gets up again. It gains on the Sheriff. Now at arm's length, he clobbers It with the rifle in Its head.
It grabs the rifle and pokes it through the Sheriff's right eye. The Sheriff falls to the paved street with blood draining down his face.
There is excessive loud radio chatter.
Law enforcement swarms. Excessive loud radio chatter is dominant. The Masked Form pounces.
A Sheriff's SUV pulls up. Three Sheriff Officers jump out armed with rifles.
They aggressively train their rifles on the Masked Form.
Bullet Shells litter.
Smoke envelops and slowly evaporates.
The Form is still standing.

SAUCE

CLICK! CLICK! CLICK!

Out of bullets.

Sheriffs back-peddle trying to get away. The Masked Form gains on them. They have reversed themselves past their cruiser and beyond.

On the roadway, an incline beckons up ahead. They see the incline, it is a steep one. TRAPPED. The Masked Form arrives knees to knees and toes to toes with them. The Masked Form grabs the rifle from Sheriff #2. He strikes him in his head. His head SPLITS open. Blood gushes out. He falls to the ground.

Sheriff #3 challenges. His body language says: *Bring it on.*

The Form does.

Now landed in the core of the Sheriff's space, defensively, the Sheriff tries to clobber It with his empty rifle. The Masked Form grabs the rifle with one hand and penetrates the Sheriff's stomach with the barrel of the weapon. The Sheriff groans and falls to the ground. Blood gushes through his back as well as his stomach.

Sheriff #4 has taken on the ascent like a Ten-Yard Dash. The Masked Form has a tremendous height advantage over the 5'6" Sheriff. They spar. The overused rifle begins to fall apart. Sensing its futility, the Sheriff discards the weapon and resorts to punch-bagging his way out of the duel.

Sirens wail in the distance.

SAUCE

The Masked Form grabs him. Spins him around. He topples to the ground. The Masked Form sticks its right foot into the vicinity of his jugular vein.
He CHOKES.
He gasps.
The Sheriff is breathless.
From the opposite direction, a Sheriff cruiser bears down. It stops on the hill. Sheriff #5 jumps out. Armed with a rifle, he fires off at The Masked Form. It dodges out of the bullets.
CLICK!
The rifle jams.
The Masked Form grabs Sheriff #5 and turns him face-down on the pitched street. It removes handcuffs from his belt. With one foot pressed firmly on the Sheriff's back, It administers the handcuffs to his wrists.
The Masked Form drags him onto the front passenger seat and fastens the seatbelt. It closes the door, picks up the gun, and heads to the driver's side of the cruiser. It opens the door and turns the engine on. Using the rifle, It places the muzzle on the gas pedal, and re-adjusting the seat backward he jams the rifle's butt between pedal and seat.
The Masked Form shuts the car door. Through that driver's window, It reaches in and slips the cruiser into drive.
The Sheriff SCREAMS.
The cruiser speedily motors downhill. Sheriff #5 fights to get his left foot accessing the pedals to no avail. The

SAUCE

Cruiser slams into a pole, rolls over multiple times, and finally flips over into a ravine.

SAUCE

38

From a distance...we hear Sheriff Chase.
"Stop it before it stops us. More than any boogeyman in our lifetimes. It is real, lethal, and dangerous. This may be the fight of your lives."
Onlookers looking at the demolition of Cops, rein themselves in.
Sheriff Chase pulls up outside the Sheriff's Department.
BRAKES SCREECH.

SAUCE

LOUD DISPATCH RADIO CHATTERS.
DOOR SLAMS.
Moments later, The Masked Form arrives outside.
Loud radio chatter reverberates.
A fleet of six Sheriff cars in landscape formation guard the huge iron gate. Two armed Sheriffs are positioned on both sides of each car. Blue and red lights rotate from all of the cruiser's roof-tops.
"Stop it before it stops us. It is real!"
Says Chase.
Other Sheriffs taunt.
The Masked Form charges.
BANG! BANG! BANG! BANG! BANG!
Bullets raining.
Additional radio chatter.
BANG! BANG! BANG! BANG! BANG!
Bullets continually rain.
Bullet Shells litter.
The Masked Form is erasable.
CLICK! CLICK! CLICK!
The Masked Form pounces toward the gate. Reloading the rifles seems futile.
The Form chuckles:
"No silver bullet, huh?"
The Sheriffs resort to clobbering It with their rifles. The Masked Form takes the hits for a minute. Suddenly, It begins tossing Sheriffs, head first to the back of their cars and their deaths.
"Stand your ground. He must fall. He will fall!"

SAUCE

Yells Sheriff Chase.

Two other SHERIFFS are left standing.

SHERIFF #16 urges:

"Bring it on! If I go down I am going to go down fighting. Because I know I can kick your ass. Even without bullets."

Sheriff #16 throws his rifle to the ground and begins attacking It with Karate moves. The Masked Form deflects all the HITS and the KICKS.

Carbon copied. The Masked Form tosses Sheriff #16 head first to the back of his car and his death.

Sheriff #17 begins to get weak-kneed. Sheriff Al Rice steps to the front with his bandaged left arm. He looks across at Sheriff #17, assured:

"Frank Cantine, if all else fails. I'll take you on. Even with my one arm. Your mother attempted cutting this off with a Chain Saw. She *choked*."

Rice looks at his left arm and continues:

"Even so, I'm still here. If Reeves doesn't take you down I F...will!"

Sheriff #17 steps up and faces The Masked Form.

"It was your mamma who did that to my boy, Al?"

He asks:

"Now you want more blood? It is my turn. A pound for a pound. Come on!"

Sheriff #17 pounds his chest. One could see **THE STREETS** in him.

"You are going down, Homes."

Sheriff #17 says.

SAUCE

He plants a few swift kicks on The Masked Form.
It deflects and challenges.
Sheriff #17 lands another swift kick which gets The Form in the groin area.
The Masked Form staggers slightly.
The handful of Sheriffs gathered - they cheer including Al Rice and Thomas Chase.
The Masked Form grabs Sheriff #17 and punches him hard in the face. He rocks backward and falls onto the pavement. It grabs his rifle and penetrates its muzzle inside his right eye socket.
He GROANS.
Dogs bark loudly.
Three attack dogs emerge hungry for the takedown of The Form.
"Who let these dogs out?"
Asks The Form.
It CHUCKLES.
Al Rice raises his hand.
The Dogs CHARGE at It.
The Masked Form stands Its ground.
The dogs cower.

SAUCE

39

Al Rice shakes off the letdown. He feels pumped and ready. He charges at The Masked Form.
It grabs Rice by his left arm and squeezes mercilessly.
He SCREAMS.
He GROANS.
The Form lifts Rice and throws him on top of the IRON gate. The pointed iron catches Rice. The spike penetrates his body.
He HANGS.
He BLEEDS.

SAUCE

In the interior of the compound a LOUD BANG reverberates.

Sissey Cantine is in a confrontation with a Sheriff Officer. He reaches for his gun. She pushes the already dislodged dual cell gate forward. The portal falls on top of the Sheriff Officer.

He kicks and bleeds.

He is lifeless.

Megan Cantine and Sissey Cantine walk out...They are focused.

The Masked Form ambles in toward them. Sheriff Chase waving his baton tries to stop Sissey and Megan Cantine.

LOUD CALCULATED FOOTSTEPS ECHO.

Chase looks back in The Masked Form's direction.

Sissey Cantine seizes the moment. She kicks Sheriff Chase hard in the left side before he can fully turn back in their direction. The Gun holster shakes loose. He falls. The Gun separates itself from the holster.

He REACHES for the fallen weapon. Megan kicks the gun out of arm's reach. Sheriff Chase is back up on his feet.

Nowhere to go, he's trapped, sandwiched. Chase resorts to hand-to-hand combat with The Masked Form.

The Form blocks his moves. It grabs him by the head and firmly twists his neck. That altercation plants him painfully onto the concrete.

SAUCE

On that warpath, the Form's mask drops off. To reveal the previously acquitted FRANK CASTILLO aka FRANK CANTINE mid-30s, mixed ethnicity.
The trio vanished into total darkness.

LATER, THE IRON GATE COLLAPSES on the opposite side of the parked cruisers. Sheriff Al Rice gets up out of the rubble.
Rice flexes his once injured left arm. Dusts himself off. Transformed, dressed in a crisp, and unstained uniform, he gets set to board a cruiser.
One can see Sheriff Thomas Chase, limping at first. Both legs are now sturdy underneath him. He upstages Rice and DARTS in the driver's seat.
Rice acknowledges his superiority and boards in the front passenger seat.
- Loud dispatch radio chatters.
Doors slam.
Engine starts.
Cruiser roars off.

About The Author

John Alan Andrews, a screenwriter, producer, playwright, director, and author of over 70 books. He has authored accounts in multiple genres: relationships, personal development, faith-based, true stories, horrors, and other vivid engaging novels. Also, a problem solver, John is sought after to address

SAUCE

success principles to young adults. He makes an impact on the lives of others, mainly because of his commitment to doing so.

Being the father of three sons propels John even more in his desire to see teens succeed. Andrews, a divorced dad of three sons Jonathan, Jefferri, and Jamison, was born in the Islands of St. Vincent and the Grenadines. His two eldest sons are also writers and wrote their first two novels while teenagers. He is elated, collaborating with Jonathan on a fourth title.

Andrews grew up in a home of five sisters and three brothers. He recounts: "My parents were all about values: work hard, love God, and never give up on your dreams."

Self-educated, John developed an interest in music. Although lacking formal education, he later put his knowledge and passion to good use, moonlighting as a disc jockey in New York. It paved the way for further exploration in the world of entertainment. In 1994 John caught the acting bug. Leaving the Big Apple for Hollywood over a decade ago not only put several national T.V. commercials under his belt but helped him to find his niche. He also appeared in the movie John Q starring Denzel Washington.

His passion for writing started in 2002 when he got denied the rights to a 1970's classic film, which he so badly wanted to remake. In 2007, while etching two of his original screenplays, he published his first book,

SAUCE

"The 5 Steps to Changing Your Life" The rest is Historic.

Currently, with several of his titles in the movie and T.V. pipeline, John is directing has to date directed two short films based on his content. Those films have won him multiple awards as well as nominations.
See IMDB: http://www.imdb.com/title/tt0854677/.

Visit: www.JohnAAndrews.com

SAUCE

OTHER RELEASES

THE UNITED STATES PANDEMIC

FIGHTING THE INVISIBLE ENEMY

FROM THE AUTHOR OF PANDEMIC WARFARE

JOHN A. ANDREWS

"A MEDICAL THRILLER"

THE AFTERMATH OF COVID - 19

SAUCE

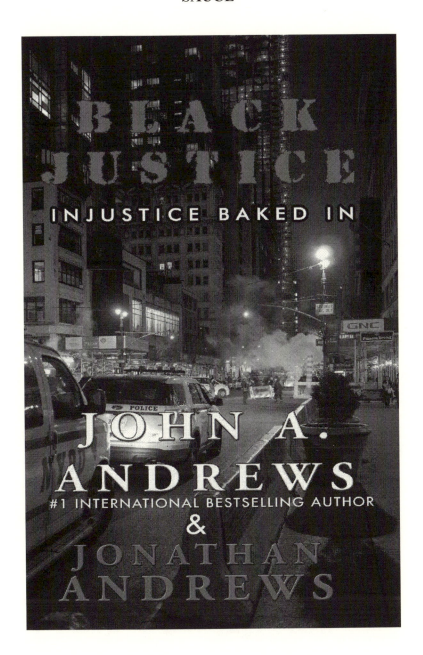

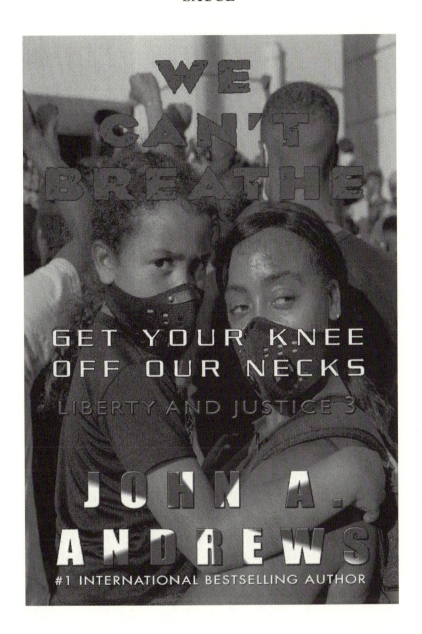

SAUCE

CHASING DESTINY

JOHN A. ANDREWS

#1 INTERNATIONAL BESTSELLING AUTHOR

GOT TO HAVE IT

SAUCE

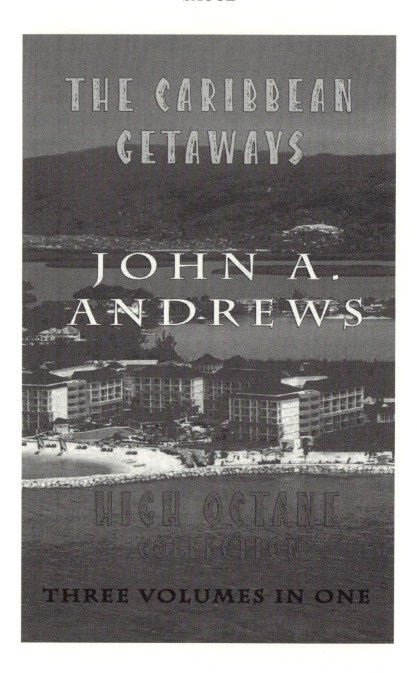

SAUCE

SAUCE

NYC

NEW YORK CONNIVERS ©

FROM THE CREATOR OF *WHO SHOT THE SHERIFF?*

JOHN A. ANDREWS

UNTIL DEATH DO US PART

A NOVEL

ONE FOOT IN **NEW YORK UNDERCOVER**
THE OTHER IN **ALFRED HITCHCOCK PRESENTS**

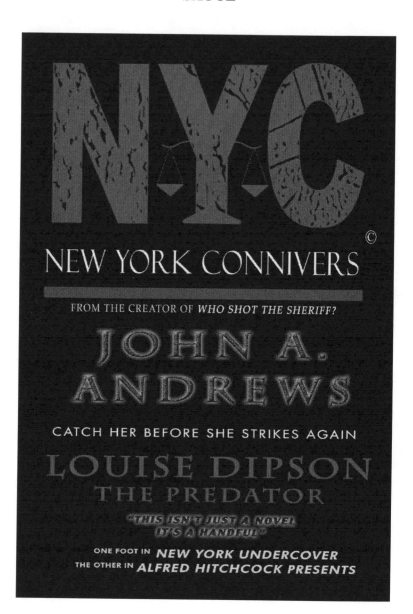

SAUCE

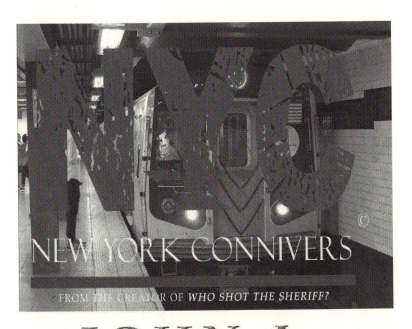

JOHN A. ANDREWS

NEW YORK CITY BLUES
THE UNDERGROUND OPERATION
A NOVEL

ONE FOOT IN *NEW YORK UNDERCOVER*
THE OTHER IN *ALFRED HITCHCOCK PRESENTS*

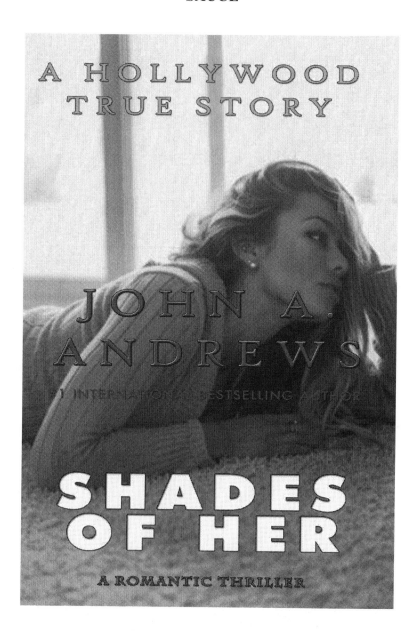

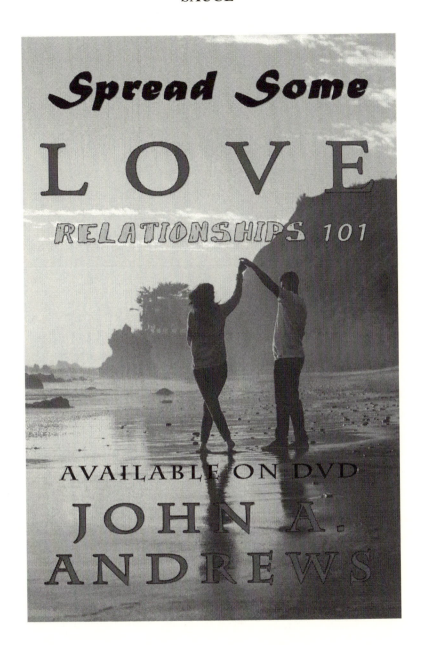

SAUCE

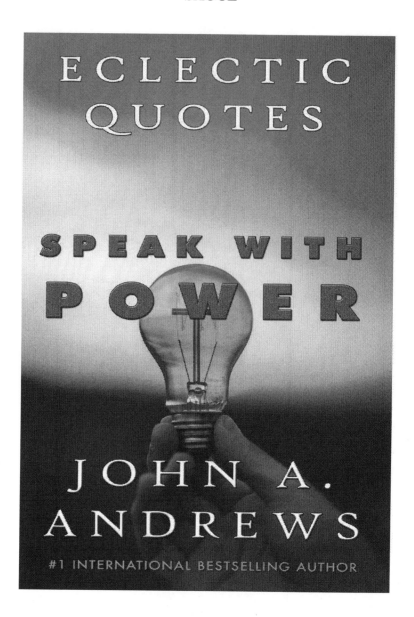

JOHN A. ANDREWS

THE MUSICAL®

FROM THE CREATOR OF
RUDE BUAY
THE WHODUNIT CHRONICLES
&
THE CHURCH ON FIRE

SO MANY ARE TRYING TO GO TO HEAVEN
WITHOUT FIRST BUILDING A HEAVEN
HERE ON EARTH...
#1 INTERNATIONAL BESTSELLER

SAUCE

THAT CONNECTS PRAISE HEAVEN & EARTH

FROM THE CREATOR OF
THE CHURCH...A HOSPITAL?

JOHN A. ANDREWS

THE CHURCH ON FIRE
THE MUSICAL®

SAUCE

JOHN A. ANDREWS
Creator of:
THE CHURCH ... A HOSPITAAL?
&
THE CHURCH ON FIRE

SAUCE

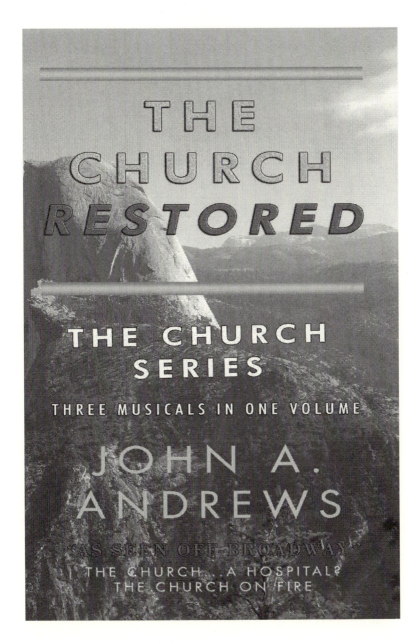

SAUCE

SAUCE

SAUCE

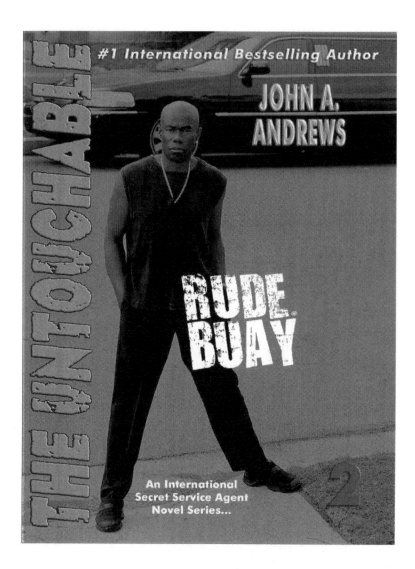

SAUCE

SAUCE

SAUCE

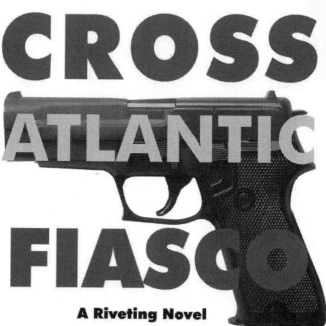

SAUCE

WHO SHOT THE SHERIFF?

The Hustle. The Flow. The Verdict.

#1 INTERNATIONAL BESTSELLER

JOHN A. ANDREWS

COMING SOON

To the Big Screen

A 2016 A L I Pictures Production

SAUCE

WHO SHOT THE SHERIFF? II

Let THE GAMES Begin...

The MILTON ROGERS' CONSPIRACY

#1 International Bestselling Author

JOHN A. ANDREWS

Co-written with Teen Authors

JONATHAN & JEFFERRI ANDREWS

SAUCE

A JOHN ANDREWS FILM

DEAD MEN TELL NO TALES

BASED ON
WHO SHOT THE SHERIFF?

WRITTEN BY: JOHN A. ANDREWS PRODUCED BY: PATRICK MCINTIRE, MICHAEL W. REID, DANIELLE E. CAMPBELL, JOHN ANDREWS
EXECUTIVE PRODUCERS: SELENA SMITH & JANIS PHILLIP
DIRECTED BY: JOHN ANDREWS. AN A L I PICTURES PRODUCTION

SAUCE

DARE TO MAKE A DIFFERENCE

SUCCESS 101

FOR

ADULTS

#1 INTERNATIONAL BESTSELLING AUTHOR

JOHN A. ANDREWS

SAUCE

SAUCE

MOMMY...
THE *MAN* FROM
THE TRAIN

FROM THE CREATOR OF
RUDE BUAY

BASED ON A TRUE STORY
BY
JOHN ALAN ANDREWS

OPTIONED FOR FILM

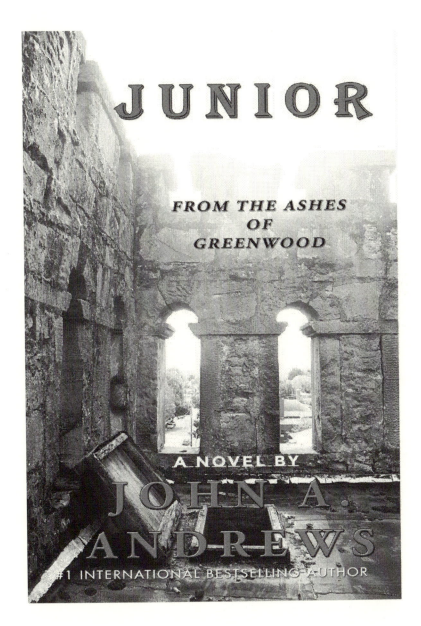

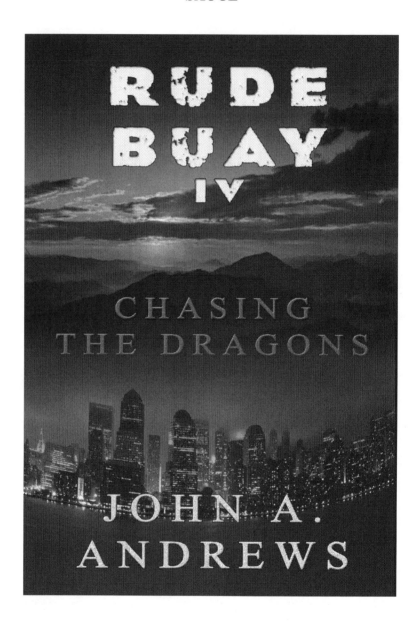

SAUCE

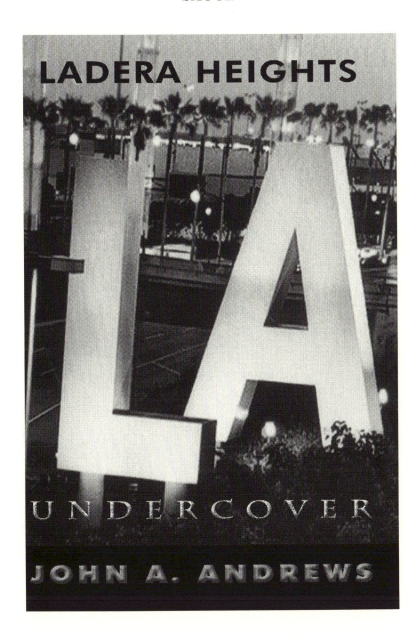

SAUCE

SAUCE

DESIREE O'GARRO
THE LETHAL KID

A TEEN THRILLER
FROM THE CREATORS OF
RUDE BUAY
AGENT O'GARRO
RENEGADE COPS
A SNITCH ON TIME
WHO SHOT THE SHERIFF?
&
THE MACOS ADVENTURE

#1 INTERNATIONAL BESTSELLING AUTHOR

JOHN A. ANDREWS
&
JEFFERRI ANDREWS

SAUCE

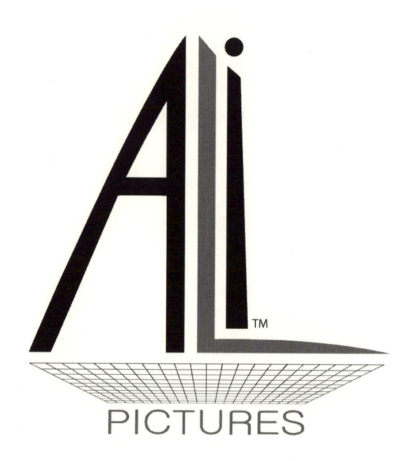

SAUCE

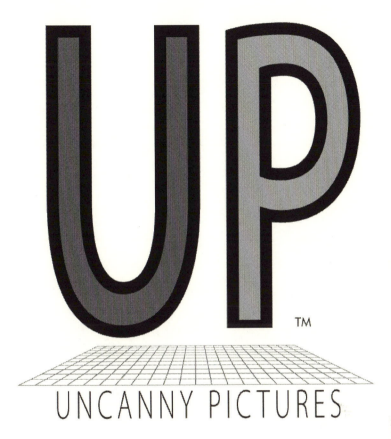

SAUCE